Joplin, Wishing

Also by Diane Stanley

The Chosen Prince

The Silver Bowl

The Cup and the Crown

The Princess of Cortova

Bella at Midnight

Saving Sky

The Mysterious Matter of I. M. Fine

The Mysterious Case of the Allbright Academy

A Time Apart

Joplin, Wishing

Diane Stanley

HARPER

An Imprint of HarperCollins*Publishers*

Joplin, Wishing
Copyright © 2017 by Diane Stanley
All rights reserved. Printed in the United States of America. No part of this book may be used or reproduced in any manner whatsoever without written permission except in the case of brief quotations embodied in critical articles and reviews. For information address HarperCollins Children's Books, a division of HarperCollins Publishers, 195 Broadway, New York, NY 10007.
www.harpercollinschildrens.com

ISBN 978-0-06-242370-2

Typography by Michelle Gengaro-Kokmen
17 18 19 20 21   PC/LSCH   10 9 8 7 6 5 4 3 2 1
❖
First Edition

In memory of my amazing mother,
Fay Grissom Stanley

Contents

1. Paparazzi   1

2. Treasure   9

3. Some Rather Unpleasant Stuff   19

4. Lucius Doyle, Antiques   30

5. A Mean Species   42

6. Show-and-Tell   52

7. Fake Apologies   58

8. Wishes   67

9. The Boy with All the Hair   77

10. The F-Word   85

11. Someplace to Live   97

12. The Short Version   105

13. The Mystery Man   114

14. Strawberry Fields   124

15. Whatever It Takes   137

16. Still Warm from the Oven   148

17. A Really Ugly Lady   160

18. What Happened Here?   175

19. A Family Thing   187

20. The Letter of the Law   202

21. Do or Die   211

22. Old and Wise   223

23. A Force to Be Reckoned With   236

Postscript: Three Years Later   245

Joplin, Wishing

1

Paparazzi

W<small>E DRAGGED INTO</small> N<small>EW</small> Y<small>ORK</small> on Friday afternoon, all wrung out from nine hours of highway driving. Mom and Aunt Jen took turns at the wheel so we could keep going straight through, stopping only for gas, bathroom breaks, snacks, and to change drivers.

Now I ask you: Who in their right mind drives from Penobscot, Maine, to New York City in a single day? Surely that's what motels are for.

To make things worse, I was crammed in the backseat with a mountain of boxes looming over me. The boxes took up most of the space, so I couldn't lie down or stretch out. Halfway through the trip, my legs started getting twitchy, and I couldn't seem to sit still. Mom kept telling me to stop fidgeting. I kept saying I couldn't. It went on like that for hour after mind-numbing hour, until we finally reached the Village and turned onto Perry Street.

I was like, *Thank you, Jesus!*

But my joy lasted exactly a nanosecond. Because right there, in front of our apartment, was this mob of reporters with cameras and microphones.

"Oh, *expletive!*" Jen groaned.

She locked all the doors and stopped at the curb. There we waited, while reporters crowded around and peered in at us, which made me feel even more claustrophobic than I already was. I bared my teeth and made animal claws at the guy outside my window. He just smirked and took my picture.

"I'm calling the police," Mom said, pulling out her cell.

"Seriously?"

"They're harassing us, Jen. And we can't unload these boxes with reporters swarming all over us."

"I guess you have a point there."

So we sat in the car, surrounded by strangers with cameras, while Mom made her call. Aunt Jen turned around and gave me a wink and a smile, which made me feel instantly better. She's good at that: cheering people up.

Just to be clear, Jen isn't really my aunt. I call her that because she feels like family. She's been Mom's best friend since their boarding school days, and I've known her all my life. Even when we lived in California, she visited us all the time. Then, after the divorce, Mom and I moved to New York. Jen's been our roommate ever since.

"Watch this," she said when Mom had finished her call. She rolled her window down a crack and shouted through the gap, "We've called the police, you vulture scum!"

The reporters were totally unimpressed. A few seemed to think it was funny. But the bottom line was, they didn't move.

Just then, through the mass of annoying reportorial bodies, I spotted Upstairs Chloe sitting on our front stoop. Chloe used to be my regular babysitter, which was very convenient since she lived right upstairs in the second-floor apartment. That's why we call her Upstairs Chloe.

That day she had on short cutoff jeans and a halter top, her go-to outfit for "catching rays." I had explained to her more than once that "catching rays" was a bad idea because it totally damaged your skin. If she kept it up she'd be wrinkled and spotted by the time she was forty. But did she listen?

Chloe had a drawing pad in her lap and seemed to be sketching the reporters. Or more likely, knowing Chloe, she was just trying to annoy them.

"Mom?" I said. "Can I go sit with Chloe?"

"Wait till the police arrive," she said. She didn't even turn around.

"I'm gonna lose my mind if I have to sit here one more minute."

Silence.

"Mom?"

"Joplin, will you *please* leave me alone?"

"Glad to!" I muttered, getting out of the car and slamming the door behind me.

The reporters moved back after I almost knocked one of them over with the door. I pushed my way through the crowd and climbed the steps.

"Hey!" Chloe said when I sat down beside her. "Wild, huh? Paparazzi on Perry Street!"

I agreed that it was wild.

Then she dropped her smile and put on a serious look. "Sorry about your grandfather," she said.

"It's okay. I'm not upset. I never actually met him."

"Really? That's weird. Was it a nice funeral?"

"We didn't have one. He left this letter for Mom saying he didn't want any kind of service. Maybe he didn't have any friends, so it'd just be a lot of crazy fans and report-ers anyway. He said Mom should feel free to throw his remains in the trash if she wanted. He didn't really care one way or the other."

"Wow, that's kind of harsh."

"Yeah, I know. Apparently he was a strange man."

"Did you? Throw his ashes away?"

I shook my head. "We scattered them in Penobscot Bay. Kind of, you know—dumped 'em in and had a moment of silence, then got back in the car. Nobody even cried."

I think Chloe was feeling a little embarrassed, hearing all that private stuff. She didn't say anything for a while after that, just went back to sketching. She drew really fast with a charcoal pencil, smudging the shadows with her finger.

I leaned over to take a look. She'd drawn several small scenes on the one big page. And though there were lots of different people in each scene, she'd grouped them together so they made a single shape. It was much more interesting that way. Maybe that was something she learned at Pratt, the art college where she was a student.

"Whoa, what's this?" Chloe said as a patrol car arrived, lights flashing.

"My mom called them. She thinks we need protection."

"Wild!"

Two officers stepped out and looked around, sizing up the situation. My mother got out of the car then and pushed her way through the scrum. The reporters went nuts, of course, taking pictures and shouting questions.

"Okay, people," one of the officers shouted. "Move along. You're being a nuisance and blocking the sidewalk."

Cameras *click-click-click*ed as they grabbed a few more quick shots of Mom with the police. Then they crossed to the other side of the street, where they continued to wait.

"What's with all the boxes in the car?" Chloe asked, busy with her pencil again. Now she was drawing my mother and the policemen.

"Papers from my grandfather's office. They were the only valuable thing in the whole place."

"Well, *I guess* they'd be valuable! Unpublished work by Martin J. Camrath? That'd be worth a fortune!"

"We don't know what's in there. Mom and Jen just shoved it all into boxes. But there sure was a lot of it."

"How come you never told me he was your grandfather?"

"Mom said not to. People get all weird when they find out. And I guess she would know."

"Joplin!" Mom called. "Come help us unload."

I was still mad and I didn't like her tone of voice, but I got up and trudged down the stairs.

"Me too," Chloe said, leaving her tablet and pencils on the stoop and following right behind. "I can tell the guys at school I helped unload Martin J. Camrath's boxes."

"Technically, the boxes weren't his," I said. "We bought them at Office Depot. It's the *contents*—"

"Oh, don't be such a little pill."

I wasn't actually trying to be a pill. Sometimes I just did it by accident.

Jen unlocked our front door while the officers stood guard on either side of the car, glaring at anyone who even thought of daring to approach. Then Mom, Jen, Chloe, and I carried box after box into the apartment, stacking them against the walls of the living room, wherever space allowed.

There was a lot of locking and unlocking of doors, like something out of a movie. I half expected guys in ninja suits to rappel down from the roof on ropes.

When we'd finished and Jen had driven off to put the car away in the garage, Mom thanked the officers and promised to send a generous donation to the police Widows' and Children's Fund.

I thought they'd leave after that, but they didn't. They seemed to be enjoying themselves. I guess helping a pretty lady, who was part of a big news story and was being hounded by paparazzi, was a lot more fun than arresting drug dealers or writing parking tickets.

"You got an alarm system?" one of them asked.

"Yes, Officer, we do."

"Good. Use it, even when you're at home."

"Hey, isn't this the block with the big garden in the middle?" the other officer said.

Mom nodded.

"Then that's a second point of entry, not visible from the street. Please tell me you don't have a sliding door."

"We don't have a sliding door."

"Good. Make sure you keep the door to the garden locked. And you might want to find a safer place for those papers, if they're as valuable as you say."

"Don't worry, Officer. I have a plan."

Finally they left. Mom smiled and waved sweetly as they drove away. Then her face sagged back to its new normal. We went inside and locked the door behind us.

2

Treasure

OUR ANSWERING MACHINE WAS FLASHING when we came in. It was a relic from the past that Mom insisted on keeping because she was fanatically careful about giving out her cell phone number. I think only five or six people had it. Everyone else called the landline. This was all about controlling her life and protecting her privacy—being the daughter of a celebrity and all.

Mom took one look at the flashing light and slumped. Why she'd be surprised, I couldn't imagine. We'd been gone a week, plus her father had just died. Of course there'd be a lot of calls.

For half a minute she stood there in front of it, scowling. Then she heaved this big, dramatic sigh you could've heard from the back row of a Broadway theater and pressed the blinking arrow.

"You have thirty-seven messages," said the robotic voice.

She pressed *stop*, sighed again, went into her bedroom, and shut the door. Leaving me standing alone in the middle of our living room, now crammed with the same annoying boxes I'd been riding with all day, and feeling completely abandoned.

I'd only wanted to go up to Penobscot, instead of staying with Upstairs Chloe, because it meant I'd get to miss a week of school. Also, I was kind of curious to see the house where Mom had lived when she was little and the room where Martin J. Camrath wrote his super-famous books. I guess that last part actually *was* kind of interesting, but mostly the trip was *not fun*, just a lot of work packing and hauling boxes, with Mom in this really foul mood the entire time.

On the drive up to Maine, she had told me I could have any of my grandfather's things I wanted. All she cared about were his papers.

I thought it would be cool to have something that had belonged to him—a set of cuff links, maybe, a watch, something small—but only because he was so famous, not for sentimental reasons. He hadn't ever been part of my life. He never came to visit us, never called, and never sent so much as a birthday card. It was almost like he'd never existed.

That first day in the Penobscot house, while Mom and Jen were packing up his office, I wandered through the rooms, searching for anything that might be of interest. But the prospects looked pretty dim. The place was old and run-down. The furniture was shabby. The rooms were damp and dark. They smelled of mildew and dust, with a hint of boiled cabbage, wet dog, and old man.

I guess when my grandparents got divorced—Mom was seven at the time—my grandmother took the pretty things with her and Martin J. never bothered to replace them. He went on living alone for the next thirty-plus years, just him and a series of Labrador retrievers, in that stripped-down, half-empty, giant, depressing old house.

There were still hooks on the walls where the pictures used to be. Couches with no lamps or side tables, bare spots with dents in the carpet from the feet of vanished chairs. If you added a few fake cobwebs and hung some rubber bats, it would have made a perfect Halloween haunted house.

In a way, I guess it really was haunted. Or at least Mom

seemed to think it was. She said it held bad memories—so bad that she refused to sleep there, though it meant we had to pay for a motel. She wouldn't go upstairs either, not even to visit her old childhood bedroom.

She said that the caretaker, Mrs. Gee, would go up there after we left and clear my grandfather's stuff away. She had no desire to see any of it.

But I was still looking for my treasure. And even though Martin J. Camrath had been a hermit, and maybe a not-nice man, maybe even a little bit crazy, he was still my grandfather. A quarter of the genes on my chromosomes came from him. And the more I thought about it, the more it seemed important to own at least one thing that had once belonged to him.

I searched the downstairs rooms but found nothing at all. The kitchen, my final stop, was especially depressing—the old chipped plates, the stained drawer liners, and the yellowing linoleum floor, curling up in places. The room felt dirty and had a slight smell of old garbage.

Eager to get away from there, I headed up the back stairs to check out the bedrooms.

There were two of them in the back, separated from the front by a laundry area and a set of double doors. I figured this must have been where the servants lived in the olden days.

Both rooms were empty. I mean completely. No rugs or furniture at all. I assumed that one of them had been my mom's, back in the 1980s. The other one, across the hall, was probably for guests.

I checked the closets. They were empty too, as was the bathroom. Not a towel, not even any toilet paper. And though it was spring, the room felt cold, like it had held on to years and years of hard winters.

The front of the house had a bathroom and two bed-rooms, one of which had been turned into a study. Books lined the shelves. There was a grungy old couch, a moth-eaten rug, and a big, soft chair. A couple of lamps. A globe. I had the feeling Martin J. hadn't used it in a long time. Like he pretty much lived in his office, ate in the kitchen, and slept in his bedroom. The rest of the house felt abandoned.

By that point it was becoming clear that if I was going to find anything interesting at all, it would be in my grandfather's bedroom. And to be honest, I wasn't too keen on going in there.

True, it was where his valuable stuff was most likely to be. But I was beginning to suspect he wasn't a cuff links and gold watch sort of guy. Also, I was creeped out by the thought of going through his stuff. I didn't want to look at his clothes, his toothbrush, his drinking glass with the lip prints still on it. He had *died* in that room just a couple of days ago. Just the sight of his bed, stripped down to the stained mattress, made me kind of sick.

Then, as I stood in the doorway trying to nerve myself up to go in, I noticed something sitting on the dresser. It caught my eye because it was red and shiny. I took a deep breath and went to have a look.

It was a round metal tin, the kind you put cakes or cookies in. There was a picture of a poinsettia on the lid.

My first thought was: *Moldy fruitcake?* It would certainly fit with everything else in that house, like the ratty old bedroom slippers and the Formica-topped kitchen table with the cigarette burns on the edge. But when I picked up the tin, I was surprised by how heavy it was. Also, it rattled, like big, hard things were sliding around inside.

I pried off the lid and sure enough it was filled with bits of broken china. Blue designs painted on white.

They were beautiful, like perfect little works of art. Each fragment was a small part of a bigger picture. I found bits of trees, the heads of some geese, a tiny windmill, part of a dress, part of a girl's face.

I knew right then that this was the thing I wanted.

I carried it downstairs to show to Mom, but she hardly

looked up. She just nodded and went back to hauling files out of the cabinet and putting them into boxes.

"Can I have it?" I asked.

"Sure. Whatever you want."

I'd felt a strange surge of pleasure then, owning that little round box with its mysterious contents. I'd held it to my chest and given it a squeeze.

Now, as I stood in our silent apartment, my mother moping behind her closed door and Jen gone off to park the car, I saw my cookie tin perched on one of the boxes.

I carried it into my room and set it on the desk. Then I sat down, removed the lid, and took the pieces out one by one. I arranged them according to subject, putting like with like, the way you do with jigsaw puzzles, except that this was a lot more interesting.

For one thing, jigsaw puzzles come with a picture on the box that shows you what they're going to look like. My puzzle was a mystery. I could tell it was some sort of country scene with a windmill, geese, and at least one girl. But the rest was yet to be revealed.

Also, my puzzle was the work of a real artist. Just touching those little bits of broken china, I felt I was in the presence of something great.

I had almost finished putting all the pieces together when I heard a click and clunk from the front of the apartment—Jen's key struggling in our ancient lock. It always took some fiddling and made a lot of noise, so I was already in the front hall by the time she opened the door.

"The vulture scum are still out there," she said, turning the deadbolt, hooking the chain latch, and pulling the shade over the front window.

"Don't tell Mom. When she heard there were thirty-seven messages on the machine, she looked like she wanted to smash it with a hammer."

"Where is she now?"

"In her room. With the door shut."

"Poor thing. She's really strung out. Those reporters were the last straw."

"Come see my picture," I said.

Jen put down her purse. She looked tired and I saw her glance over at my mom's door. I could tell she really wanted to go in there and comfort her, acting more like my mother's mother than her best friend.

"*Please?* It'll just take a second."

"All right, sweet thing," she said, rumpling my hair, which I mostly hated because hair rumpling was something you did to little kids, and I was almost twelve. But it also felt good because there was love in it, and I needed some love just then.

"What's this?" Jen said when I led her to my desk.

I still had some work to do on the design around the edges, but the scene was completely finished. There was a pond with lots of trees around it, their branches swaying in the wind. The sky was full of fluffy clouds, and there was a windmill off in the distance. But front and center was a girl standing beside the pond with a little flock of geese. She had a sweet face and pale hair that she wore in braids.

The artist had painted her very carefully, like a portrait. I felt as though I'd know her if I passed her on the street.

"Isn't it pretty?" I said.

"It's wonderful," she agreed.

"I'm not sure what it is. Some kind of really big plate."

"It's a platter, hon—like what you'd put the turkey on at Christmas." She leaned over and studied it more carefully. "Wow, Joplin. This is very fine work."

"I'm going to glue it back together."

"Horrors! Don't you dare!"

"Why?"

"You'll make a hash of it—so would I—and it's a valuable antique. It needs to be done by an expert. If you want, I can take you to this shop I know on Bedford Street. They repair all kinds of old treasures."

"Can we go tomorrow?"

"Sure. We'll do it first thing. Now I need to go look in on your mom."

She went to Mom's door, leaned against the jamb, and gave a quick little double knock with her left hand. "Annie?" she said.

Mom peered out, looking gray and kind of feeble.

"I have some instructions for you." Jen made herself sound like the bossy teacher everybody hates.

"And what might they be?"

"You are to draw a nice hot bath and add a few drops of lavender oil. Then you are to find a really mindless, trashy book, get in the aforementioned bath, and read till you're wrinkled like a prune. Am I clear?"

"Bath. Oil. Book. Prune. Got it."

"While you're doing that, I'll play the phone messages and delete all the garbage. I'll make a list of any that apply to you and save them if appropriate. Then Joplin and I will go into the kitchen and scrounge up some dinner. Okay?"

"You're an angel."

"I know. I get that all the time."

3

Some Rather
Unpleasant Stuff

I SPRAWLED OUT ON THE couch, eyes closed, and listened while Jen went through the messages. I'll admit I held out the faint, foolish hope that one of the calls might be for me. But mostly I was there because I didn't want to be alone.

A lot of the messages were hang-ups—probably reporters trying to catch my mom at home. A few of them even left messages.

"Why, of course Mrs. Danforth will call you *right* back," Jen would say as she hit *erase*, cutting them off in midsentence.

Then there were the usual reminders from the dentist and the hair salon. And sandwiched in between them were condolence calls from friends. All very nice, all pretty much the same: They were sorry for our loss.

I was almost asleep when I heard my dad's voice.

"Anne—it's Tom. I just heard about your father. I can only imagine how hard this must be for you." In the background I could hear the shrieking of children: Harrison and Judith, the Feral Twins.

"You're probably up in Maine now, so I won't bother you on your cell. I'll try again next week. I just wanted to say it in person—you know, how sorry I am. Bye now. Be strong."

Jen scribbled on her pad.

Three more messages followed: two hang-ups and a squealy-voiced robo-woman announcing that we'd won a free trip to Florida.

We won that trip a lot. Jen assured me it wasn't something we ever wanted to do. She said they fly you there for free, then put you in a room and talk to you nonstop until you're so worn down and hungry and tired that you agree to buy a time-share.

Bored, I got up and headed for my room. I was just about to close the door when I heard Dad's voice again.

"Hi, it's me. Sorry to call you back so soon, but I wanted

to warn you, in case you've been too busy to follow the news. There's some . . . *rather unpleasant* stuff about your father online. I hope you'll make sure that Joplin doesn't see it. You probably don't want to see it either. Anyway, I thought I'd better give you the heads-up. Hang in there. Talk to you later."

I slipped into my room, had my computer open on my lap, and was already Googling *Martin J. Camrath* when Jen suddenly appeared. She plopped down beside me on the bed and shut the laptop, practically crushing my fingers.

"Ow! Could you at least let me get my hands out first?"

"Serves you right," she snapped. "Your dad calls to warn your mom about cruel and hurtful trash online—and says he *particularly* doesn't want you to look at it. So the first thing you do is come in here and start searching the internet?"

"The kids at school will've seen it and I'll have to deal with it. I need to know."

"That's ridiculous. They're fifth graders. They've never even heard of Martin J. Camrath."

"His obituary was in all the papers. Mom said."

"Your friends read the obituaries in the *New York Times*?"

"*No*. But their parents do, especially if it's somebody famous. And one of them is sure to recognize our names.

Then the mom or dad will say, 'Hey, Brittany! Does the name Joplin Danforth ring a bell? Isn't she that really weird girl in your class?' And Brittany will say, 'Yes, Mom or Dad, I totally despise her. Why?' And Mom or Dad will say, 'She's Martin J. Camrath's granddaughter!' Then Brittany will say, 'Who's that?' and—"

"I get it, Joplin."

"—and Brittany will call Kimberly and say, 'Guess what!'"

"Stop!"

"I just need to find out, okay? I know he was strange, the way he never left the house and all. But from what my dad said, this is a lot worse. Was he crazy or something?"

"No, Joplin, he was not crazy. Your grandfather was a brilliant writer who was . . . a little eccentric."

"Like Einstein?"

"Exactly! Einstein didn't wear socks, he was always rumpled, and his hair was a mess. But he was also a great genius. Just like your grandfather. You might use that analogy if the kids tease you at school."

"Oh, right. Like that'll really impress them."

"Suit yourself. But whatever you do—" Jen stopped suddenly, blinked, and went to look out the window. Two guys in business clothes were walking in the garden, which was totally weird.

"Joplin, have you ever seen those men before? You're out in the garden all the time."

"No. I'm usually the only person there. Sometimes there are nannies with little kids. But those two—they're definitely suspicious."

"They must live in one of the brownstones. How else could they have gotten in?"

This was true. The garden was private, an enormous, block-long green space shielded from the streets on all four sides by rows of town houses, plus the Episcopal church across the way.

The men were coming closer now, following a gravel path between low boxwood hedges that ran parallel to our block. They stopped for half a minute to admire one of the fountains, then took a right turn and strolled casually in the direction of our back door.

"That is *so* fake!" I said just as one of the men held a pocket-size camera up to his face and snapped.

"Oh!" Jen gasped. Then she was off like a flash, out of my room and into hers. I heard her scrabbling around in her closet, then the sound of the back door opening. And suddenly there she was, in the garden, running at the two men like a maniac, a golf club in her right hand raised like a weapon.

Their reaction was pretty hilarious.

First there was this startled expression, like *whaaaaa?*

Then they locked glances, as in *yikes!*

And then they were off like a couple of rockets, dashing toward the church's back door, leaping over hedges, nearly colliding with a stone lion. They made it inside with inches to spare.

But if they thought that was the end of it, they were seriously mistaken. Jen went right in after them. Five minutes later she reappeared, merrily swinging her golf club and looking very smug.

She can be totally adorable sometimes.

"Had a few words with the church secretary," she said when she came back, somewhat out of breath. "She'll be keeping the garden door locked from now on." She put her golf club away in its bag and led me back to my room. Once again we sat side by side on my bed.

"Where were we? Oh yes. Brittany and Kimberly."

"You think it's funny, but you don't know how mean kids can be. And if I go back to school totally clueless—"

"I *do* know how mean kids can be. Adults too. We're a mean species. Which is why your father, and your mother, and your dear auntie Jen *are trying to protect you.*"

"I need to know."

"Okay, listen—it's probably just some unflattering photos. Like, someone snuck onto his property and waited around in the bushes for Martin to take out the trash. Maybe one time he went out in his skivvies. And while he was out there, let's say the wind blew his hair up so it looked really wild. And maybe he heard a rustling in the bushes, and saw the photographer, and yelled at him. And *that's* when the guy snapped his picture. Now they're running the photo with a story saying he was crazy. I'm making this up, but I'm probably close."

I nodded. That's what paparazzi did. They took embarrassing pictures of famous people and made money selling them.

"So here's what I suggest. You promise not to go looking on your own. I'll do some research. Then I'll give you a full report. Okay? Is that a deal?"

I nodded again.

"Good girl. Now, we don't want to make things any worse for your mom than they already are. I'll talk to her about this later. Can you *please* not bring this up over dinner?"

"All right."

"Oh, Joplin—don't *you* go crying on me now!"

"I'm not crying." I wiped my eyes with the back of my hand and sniffed.

"Of course not. My mistake. What's say we go grill some cheese?"

We ate on our laps in the living room, Mom in her night-gown and robe, Otis Redding on the stereo. We were all mellow and into the ice cream before Mom thought to ask about the messages.

Jen shot me a warning glance. "Tom called. He just wanted to say he was sorry. Said he'd call back."

"That was nice."

"He's a nice man. Always was."

Mom didn't respond. Whatever went wrong between them, she never bad-mouthed him in front of me.

"The rest was the usual. I saved the reminders and condolence calls. Nothing urgent."

"Good." She pressed her lips together, a nervous habit when she was thinking. "Jen, I called Jackson Sloan about the papers. He was wonderful."

"Of course he was. If there's anything in those boxes that even remotely resembles a novel, it'll sell a million copies. If it's any good, it'll sell twenty million. You could have held an auction, you know. Then Jackson would've had to bid for it."

"Why would I do that? Sloan, Hart was always Dad-dy's publisher. And Jackson is an old friend. I want him to publish the books if there's anything of value. He'll do it right. And honestly, Jen—I can't handle this alone. I need to be involved, but it would take me years to read and organize it all."

"I know."

"Also, I want Dad's papers out of here. They need to be someplace safe. Jackson's coming over at ten tomorrow to pick them up. He's hiring an armored truck, if you can believe it. And people to carry the boxes."

"Awesome!" I said. "Can I tell Upstairs Chloe?"

"I told him about the reporters," Mom went on, as if I hadn't just asked a question. "He said he was going to call a security company and get some agents out here to watch our apartment. Just for a while, till things cool down."

"Don't you think they'll leave us alone once they see that the papers are gone?"

"I doubt it. They still want to interview me."

"Of course. Modern journalism at its best: 'Mrs. Danforth, how did you *feel* when you heard that your father had died?'" She shoved an imaginary microphone in Mom's direction and did a fake-Mom voice. "'I felt really crappy.'" Then both arms wide like a banner headline: *"Breaking News! Daughter of Martin J. Camrath Feels Sad!"*

Jen could usually make people laugh, and she was trying really hard this time. But Mom just sighed. "Anyway, Jackson thought we should have some protection."

"What's it going to cost us?"

"Nothing. He's paying for it."

"You mean Sloan, Hart is paying."

"No, Jackson himself, out of his own pocket. He said to think of it as a gift."

"My, my!" Jen flashed a wicked grin. "He sure knows how to woo a girl—armored trucks, box schleppers, *security guards*!"

"Nonsense," Mom said. "This is just business."

"Oh, right. Business."

"Anyway, I really hate to ask this after everything you've already done, but are you working tomorrow?"

"Not till Monday, why?"

"Well, once they've picked up the boxes, I need to go up to the Sloan, Hart offices. Jackson's rounding up a team of editorial assistants as we speak, to organize and catalog the papers. They'll all be on hand and I need to approve the storage space and set the ground rules. No taking anything out of the room, no one ever alone in there, that sort of thing."

"Sounds like a caper movie," I said. And once again my mind went to ninjas on ropes, only this time the scene involved a sixty-story building and crashing through a plate-glass window. "Can I call Chloe now?"

"It'll take me most of the day, I'm afraid."

"Not to worry," Jen said. "As it happens, Joplin and I were just planning an all-day excursion to—where was it again, sweetie?"

"Paris?"

"Right. Paris."

"Ah. Well, bon voyage then."

4

Lucius Doyle, Antiques

It was a quarter to ten. I sat with Chloe on the front stoop while she took pictures of the reporters across the street, zooming in on individual faces.

"They look *so* bored," she muttered (*click, click*). "And I am irritating them *so* much. They keep giving me dirty looks."

"Good," I said.

Jackson Sloan pulled up in a little blue car, arousing the photographers' interest. He had on pressed jeans and a crisp white shirt. His loafers were really shiny. He reminded me of the guy in that magazine ad—you know, the handsome older man who wants to pass his Rolex down to his son? Or probably it was his grandson.

Mom came out to meet him and they stood together on the sidewalk. I couldn't hear what they were saying, but he put his hand on her shoulder while they talked.

"Jen thinks he likes my mom."

"*Really?*" Chloe put her camera down. "You mean likes as in *likes?*"

"Yeah."

"She could do a lot worse. Cute guy. Nice car."

"Yeah. His family owns a publishing company."

"Better still."

Jen came out to join them just as Jackson's cell phone rang. He held it to his ear and nodded. Then moments later a boxy white truck turned a corner and headed our way. It looked like a military vehicle. Probably had bulletproof glass.

"That is *so* awesome!" Chloe said, behind her camera again, clicking away. Across the street, the press had parted like the Red Sea, scattering in both directions in hopes of getting an angle where the truck wouldn't block their view.

Chloe and I had the best seats of all.

Two guards hopped out of the truck. They wore dark blue uniforms with gold buttons and official-looking badges. I knew they weren't real police, just fancy rent-a-cops, but they had guns and looked plenty intimidating. They even shot suspicious looks in our direction.

"It's okay," Jen said. "They're family." I saw Chloe grin at that from behind her camera.

Next came the box schleppers, four pumped-up guys in a Toyota van. They scurried over to Jackson Sloan, who gave them their instructions. Then, with the guards protecting the perimeter and Jen inside the apartment showing them what to take, they cleared all the boxes from our living room and loaded them into the truck. It took them half the time it had taken us to carry them in—maybe fifteen minutes from start to finish.

The guards locked up, which was something of a production, then hopped into the cab and drove away. The box schleppers followed in their van. Mom and Jackson Sloan brought up the rear, following the procession uptown to the publishing office.

"It's all over, vulture scum," Jen shouted gaily to the reporters. "You can go home now."

They ignored her, of course. They were busy with their phones, calling in the story, alerting their vulture masters to send some more people over to Sloan, Hart, where the show would begin its second act.

Jen turned to me. "You ready, Joplin?"

"Yup."

"Where're you going?" Chloe asked.

"To some antiques shop where they fix broken things."

"Oh," she said. "Great. I'm going back to bed."

We stood outside Lucius Doyle, Antiques ("Repairs and Restoration"), looking in the window through the security shutters. A man inside was flicking on lights, bustling around, getting ready to open.

"Looks pretty fancy," I said. Everything inside either sparkled or gleamed—cut crystal, old wood, silver and gold. It reminded me of my former best friend Abby's house, with the teardrop crystal chandeliers, and the gilded ceiling, and all kinds of precious stuff we weren't allowed to touch.

"It's fancy, all right," Jen said. "But the important thing is that Lucius Doyle is a true artist at restoration. He knows about the materials people used five hundred years ago—old glue, varnishes, that sort of thing. He'll do a proper job."

The man was at the door now, unlocking it. We stood back while he rolled up the metal shutters. Then he invited us in.

"Mr. Doyle, I'm Jennifer Moss. I work at Christie's. We've met before."

"Good to see you again." He glanced down at me and my cookie tin. I had the feeling children weren't especially welcome at Lucius Doyle, Antiques.

"What can I do for you, Ms. Moss?"

"Joplin here has a treasure she would like to have repaired."

There was a heavy pause. He was probably imagining a doll that had lost its head.

"What sort of treasure?"

"I'm guessing it's a very old delftware platter. Not my area of expertise, but you would know. It's badly broken, I'm afraid."

Lucius Doyle suddenly seemed much more interested. "Let's take it over to my desk," he said. "We'll give it a good look-see."

We followed him down a pathway between tables, all of them groaning with precious, old, super-expensive things that Abby's mother would die for. I gripped the cookie tin and pulled in my elbows, making myself as small and harmless as possible.

At the back of the room was a large desk, probably antique. Lucius Doyle took his place behind it and we sat across from him.

He was a short, solid man with a funny haircut and a bulbous nose. On the index finger of his right hand he wore a big gold ring with a square blue stone. There was a smaller one with a red stone on his pinkie. I figured they must be antique rings, so he'd put them on whatever fingers they fit.

Jen took the cookie tin and set it in front of Mr. Doyle. He touched the lid, right in the yellow center of the red poinsettia. "Sears, 1957," he said. When we both looked confused, he laughed. "My apologies. A feeble joke. May I open it?"

"Sure," I said.

He worked off the lid and set it aside. Then, very carefully, he took out the broken shards, putting each in its proper place as I had done the day before. Except that he did it faster, as if he already knew where the pieces went.

Finally, Mr. Doyle turned on this strange sort of gooseneck lamp. It had a ring-shaped fluorescent light with a magnifying glass in the center. He kept changing the angle of the glass so he could study every part of the platter.

At last he moved the magnifying light aside and just sat there staring at the scene laid out before him—the trees, grass, and little windmill, the pond, the flock of geese, and the girl.

Lucius Doyle was breathing pretty hard by then, the

way old people do when they climb stairs. But he wasn't old, more like middle-aged. And he was sitting down, not climbing stairs. I could tell he was trying to control the heavy breathing, like he was embarrassed by it.

"What do you think?" Jen asked.

"You were correct," he said. "This is delftware from Holland, probably mid-seventeenth century." Then to me, "That means approximately 1650."

"I know what *seventeenth century* means."

"Good. So how did it come into your possession?"

His skin was flushed. He was gleaming with sweat, though it wasn't hot in there.

"It belonged to my grandparents," I said. "My mother gave it to me."

"Well." He was really struggling to breathe now. I wondered if maybe he was having a heart attack. I was pretty sure that sweating and agitation were two of the symptoms. "It's badly broken, as you can see. And that's a pity. It would have been highly collectible in its original condition. But as it is now, it's worth nothing."

"I don't care," I said. "I just want it fixed. You can do that, right?"

"Of course. But that won't restore its value."

"I know. That's all right."

He was looking down again, touching the broken bits

of pottery as if stroking a kitten, tracing the delicate lines drawn in blue. "But you know, this really is quite charming. I wouldn't be surprised if it was the work of Hans van der Brock. I'd have to do some research to confirm it, but my instinct tells me this is so. The quality of the portraiture and the absence of a factory mark support it."

"Is he somebody famous?" I asked.

"Not really. Only to connoisseurs of antique porcelain. He was an unusually gifted artist."

I turned to Jen. "Have you ever heard of him? Hans van der Brock?"

"No, hon. But that doesn't mean anything. Painting's my subject, not ceramics."

"I wonder," Lucius Doyle said, looking directly at me, "if you might be willing to sell it? I would give you a hundred dollars. That's a very good price for a broken platter. You can ask Ms. Moss if you have any doubt that it's a fair offer. But I have always wanted to own a Van der Brock, even a broken one. And it would cost you twice that to repair it."

I looked at Jen, shocked. *"Two hundred dollars?"*

"Don't worry, Joplin. That's pretty much what I was expecting. And he'll do an expert job."

"But I don't have two hundred dollars."

"Relax. This is my treat. It's really not a big deal."

"Okay. But I don't want to sell it. Just fix it, please."

Lucius Doyle opened a drawer and took out a form. He asked for my name, address, and phone number. His writing was beautiful—fancy and swirly in an old-fashioned way, like on the Declaration of Independence.

"Are you sure you won't reconsider? I can't imagine what a little girl like you would do with a damaged old platter."

"I'd look at it. I think it's beautiful."

"I think so too. How would it be if I offered you five hundred?"

"Dollars?"

"Yes."

I sat there blinking stupidly, stunned by the amount. I didn't know what to do.

Also, something about Lucius Doyle was really bothering me.

"No, thank you," I said in a whisper.

"As you wish. But if I'm really pleased with the restoration, I might be willing to offer you more than five hundred. Maybe then you'll change your mind."

"Actually," I said, "I *have* changed my mind."

Doyle drew a quick breath, as if he was about to say something, but then he didn't. He just looked at me expectantly, his head cocked to the side.

"I've decided I *don't* want it repaired."

"Are you sure?" Jen and Lucius Doyle said at the exact same time.

"Yes." My voice was trembling. "I . . . it's more fun to play with the way it is. I can put it together like a puzzle." I shot Jen a pleading look. She gave me the tiniest nod.

"Oh dear," she said, getting to her feet. "I'm so sorry, Mr. Doyle. I'm afraid we've wasted your time. But children, you know—they have the most curious notions. And it *is* her special treasure. I suppose she can do whatever she wants with it."

All this time, while she was nattering on about how silly children were, Jen was collecting the pieces and putting them back into the cookie tin. Lucius Doyle just stared, frozen with astonishment, apparently unable to speak.

"Thank you for being so patient and understanding."

Jen had the lid on now and the cookie tin firmly in hand.

"I'll talk to her about it," she added, as if I weren't standing right there listening to everything she said. "Maybe she'll come around."

We left in a more or less civilized manner. But once outside, we raced down the sidewalk, looking over our shoulders like a pair of escaping ninjas. Not till we reached the corner did we stop to catch our breaths.

"You think I'm crazy," I said.

"No. You were way ahead of me. I couldn't get past his reputation. He's so well respected in the art world. But you were noticing other things, and you were right. Lucius Doyle wasn't being straight with us."

"What do you mean?"

"He kept saying how worthless the platter was, yet he was so insistent about wanting to buy it. You hear stories all the time about antiques dealers who buy some dirty old picture for fifty bucks and it turns out to be a Turner or a Rembrandt. He had that air about him, like he'd just hit the jackpot. And he was trying so hard not to show it."

"Yeah. He was sweating and his hands were shaking. But that's not why I wanted to leave. I just really, really didn't trust him. He gave me the shivers. Like he was the devil in disguise or something."

"That's going a bit too far. But I assure you, we won't go back."

"Good." When the light changed, we crossed the street for no particular reason. We still didn't have a plan. "So you think my platter might be worth something?"

"Could be. I'll ask around at work, see if anyone's heard of Hans van der Brock. But for now I think we should take it back to the apartment and wrap the pieces in tissue, then put it away in a safe place."

"I don't want to put it away. I want to hang it on my wall with one of those plate-hanger thingies, so I can look at it whenever I want."

"Positive?"

"Absolutely. Is there someone else who would do a good job? Besides Lucius Doyle?"

"Yes. A very sweet lady on the Upper East Side who doesn't even remotely look like the devil."

"Perfect," I said. "Let's go."

5

A Mean Species

I slipped into homeroom on Monday morning, keeping my head down, avoiding eye contact, and generally trying to make myself invisible. It didn't work, of course. The whole class stopped whatever they were doing and turned to stare at me.

You'd think I'd come to school naked.

My first, instinctive thought was of Abby. And for one brief, pitiful moment I actually imagined her seeing how miserable I was, throwing off the evil spell that had turned her into a mean girl, and defying her new clique of designer-purse-carrying Fashionistas just long enough to come over and give me a hug.

I looked straight at her, willing her to do it. But she didn't. She just gazed down at her neon blue fingernails, like they were the most interesting things in the world.

"Joplin," the teacher said, "will you come here a moment?"

Going to stand with the teacher in front of the whole class was the very last thing I wanted to do. But I had no choice. So I trudged back up the path between two rows of desks and stood beside Ms. Warrick, waiting.

She draped an arm gently over my shoulders and pulled me closer, giving me a little squeeze. "I'm so sorry for your loss," she said. "Your grandfather was a remarkable writer, as I'm sure you already know."

I noticed how she pitched her voice just low enough that it sounded like a private conversation, yet loud enough for everyone to hear. This wasn't just for me; it was for the whole class.

"I read *All the Fanfare, All the Lights* when I was in college and it really rocked my world. Camrath was still a cult author back then and those of us who read him felt, you know, really sophisticated and ahead of the curve. Then he won the Pulitzer and was on the cover of *Time*, and our so-called secret was out. He's in the pantheon now. You must be terribly proud of him."

I muttered something. She squeezed my shoulder again. But as I went back to my seat, I noticed the mood had changed.

One point for clever, kindhearted teachers.

But ten points for forgetful students. Because by the time we'd left homeroom, prizewinning and world-rocking were ancient history. Kids I didn't even know stared and pointed at me in the hall. They whispered to their friends, who snickered. Then from the crowd I started hearing animal sounds—mostly dog growls and barks, though there was also the occasional ape call.

Exactly what I'd been afraid of.

Jen's guess about the "rather unpleasant stuff" had been amazingly accurate. There were "crazy recluse" stories, with pictures of my grandfather looking unkempt and unwashed. There were "wild man" stories, showing him outside in his underwear with his hair all over the place. But when Jen *very reluctantly* showed me the worst one of all, I knew that life as I'd known it was over.

The "reporter" had apparently gone through my grandfather's garbage can and found some empty dog food cans in there. He conveniently ignored the fact that my grandfather also owned a dog. So the headline read: "WILDMAN AUTHOR CAMRATH LIVED ON DOG FOOD."

Naturally there was a photo to prove it. He was out in the yard on his hands and knees (wearing pants this time). I don't know what he was doing—pulling weeds, maybe, or looking for something he'd dropped. But it didn't matter, because they'd Photoshopped a dog bowl into the picture so it looked like he was about to chow down on a nice warm pile of Liver 'n' Kidney Delight.

Obviously someone had found the site and forwarded the link to half the school.

Hence the barks and growls.

As Jen said, we're a mean species.

When the bell finally rang for middle school lunch, I almost fainted with relief. It meant I could go to the library, where, for a full fifty-five minutes, no one would bother me.

This was nothing new. The library had been my refuge since September. That's when Abby, all tan and rosy from two months on Martha's Vineyard, had dropped her little bomb.

We'd been "drifting apart," she explained in this weird, preachy, obnoxious voice. We "didn't have that much in common" anymore, so there was "no point in dragging it out." Maybe it would be better just to "rip off the bandage, get it over with, and go our separate ways."

Now, I've known Abby Strasser since we were four years old, and that's not how Abby talks.

That's how *her mother* talks. And her mother never liked me.

Mrs. Strasser thought I was "kind of scruffy" because I wore jeans a lot.

She thought I was "peculiar" because of the way I talk—that is to say, I use big words.

Also because I was "named after a drug addict," which I guess is technically true if you only count Janis Joplin.

She said my life was "unstable" because my parents were divorced and Mom "couldn't even afford a basement apartment unless she shared it with a roommate." That last bit was total garbage. We *own* our apartment. Mom inherited it from her mother. And Jen lives with us because we love her.

In short, Mrs. Strasser felt that I was "not the sort of person" Abby should be friends with, because it would "harm her socially."

I knew all this because Abby had told me. I guess it didn't occur to her that hearing all those mean things might hurt my feelings. Which of course it did. But it didn't hurt *too* much because we laughed about it together. We made fun of the way Mrs. Strasser talked with her lips pursed, and how she walked around with her nose in the air so people wouldn't notice her double chin. We called her grand double brownstone with the butler and the gilded ceiling the "Palatial Mansion," PM for short. And we called my place the SBA for "Squalid Basement Apartment."

Abby had her feet on the ground back then. We took something ugly and had fun with it.

I guess it's to her credit that she stuck with me as long as she did. But once she'd bought the line her mother had been selling for years, it was sudden and shocking. Worse, I found myself totally out in the cold because Abby was the only friend I had—except for Jen, who was practically middle-aged, and Chloe, who was a college student.

So I spent what free time I had at school with the librarian, Ms. Finney, and a handful of nameless nerds, all of us keeping politely to ourselves. It was lonely and pathetic, but at least it felt safe.

I couldn't wait to get there.

I headed for my usual table in the far right corner, half hidden by the last row of the nonfiction section, and settled in to eat my lunch in peace.

The next thing I knew, Ms. Finney was sitting down beside me.

I was holding a partially eaten peanut-butter-and-banana sandwich, and we weren't supposed to bring food into the library. Ms. Finney pretended not to notice.

"I'm so sorry about your grandfather," she said, like all my teachers. A memo must have gone out to the staff, designating Monday as "Be Kind to Joplin Day."

I nodded and put on a fake smile, as I'd been doing all morning. Next she'd tell me how my grandfather's work had transformed her life.

"Have you ever read any of his books?" she asked.

"No. My mom said to wait till I'm older."

"She's right, of course. But I'm kind of sorry, because I think it would help if you understood how truly amazing he was."

"Um," I said, suddenly aware that we were being watched. Ms. Finney followed my gaze.

"What is it, Barrett?"

He was one of the regulars, a tall boy with lots of dark, curly hair. He was standing at a polite distance, hands folded, waiting to get Ms. Finney's attention.

"Sorry. I just wanted to ask if *The Hound of the Baskervilles*—"

"Not back yet. I *promise* to let you know the minute it comes in. I won't let anyone else check it out."

"Thanks. Sorry to interrupt." He backed away apologetically.

"*Huge* Sherlock Holmes fan," Ms. Finney whispered.

"Me too. Maybe he could borrow ours. We have the whole set."

This was true; we did have the whole set. But I only said that to change the subject. I was really, really sick of talking about Martin J. Camrath.

Ms. Finney tilted her head and gave me this very odd look. And I was wishing she wouldn't do that, because it made me feel weird, when the door opened and a crowd of fifth graders came piling in.

Travis and Ryan were in the lead, followed by three or four other boys. Trailing behind were the Fashionistas, giggling softly. They were looking around in this totally dopey way, like they weren't sure what a library was for.

But I knew better. They were looking for me.

The minute Ms. Finney turned her head, I swept the remains of my sandwich off the table and into my lap. When I looked up again, it was clear they had spotted me.

Ms. Finney, who wasn't born yesterday, guessed what was about to happen. So she got to her feet and stood, arms crossed, blocking the path to my table.

"What can I do for you?" she asked.

Travis was glowing with that stupid joy known only to bullies who are about to play a *really awesome* prank.

"We're looking for a book," he said with this face-splitting grin.

"Well, you came to the right place. Any particular subject?"

Travis couldn't control himself. He barely got it out before he started laughing. "Something about the abdominal snowman!"

The crowd went wild. Snorts and guffaws.

"You mean *abominable*, right?"

Apparently that was the funniest thing that any of them had ever heard. They totally lost it, spewing snot and spit, choking and coughing, laughing so hard I was afraid one of them might throw up on the carpet.

"Why don't you try the Lower School library?" Ms. Finney said. "Look in the *picture book* section."

That just made it worse. Travis was now incapable of speech, so Jason took over. "Anything on *the Wolf-Man*?" he asked.

All this time I'd been searching for Abby but hadn't found her. If she was there, which I hoped with all my heart she was not, she must have been hidden in the back of the crowd.

It would be easy for her to do. Abby was about the size of a peanut.

Suddenly, there was a loud *slam*!

I jumped.

The boy with all the hair jumped.

So did the kid with the huge stack of Harry Potter books and the girl who always did her math over lunch.

Travis jumped and Celine went, "Eeeek!"

Then it was just shocked silence.

Ms. Finney, who had dropped a dictionary onto her desk from about shoulder height, had definitely gotten their attention.

She was still smiling, but her voice was as hard as ice. "Now, I want you *little children* to take your infantile jokes and appalling manners out of my library. And you may not come back, not even to do research for a school assignment, until you've brought me a note of apology signed by your parents."

As they turned to go, giggling nervously, I caught a flash of chestnut hair at the back of the crowd. I saw her face for just a second.

And then she was gone.

6

Show-and-Tell

I GOT TO MATH JUST before the bell. Everyone else was already there, seated and waiting for class to start. Mr. Crocker didn't look up. As usual, he was grading papers.

I could tell something was up, though. It was much too quiet in there. And as I made my way down the row of desks, I spotted more than one tight-lipped, wicked grin. Finally I got to my seat, and I swear every student in the room stopped breathing.

This was the moment they'd been waiting for.

A pyramid of dry dog food had been neatly arranged on my desk.

Unlike the barks and growls and the scene in the library, this little prank had been planned in advance. Someone had scooped the pellets into a baggie, put the baggie into his backpack, and carried it to school. Worse, I saw that there were three or four different brands, varying in color, shape, and size. That meant it had been a group effort, several people bringing whatever they had at home. There would have been phone calls to hatch the plot and work out the details. Which class? How should they do it? Wouldn't it be hi-*larious*?

All of that, just to humiliate me.

I was so heartsick I couldn't move. I couldn't leave. I was frozen to the spot.

Then the bell rang.

"Okay, class," Mr. Crocker said. "Time to get started."

Was it possible he hadn't noticed—me still standing in the aisle, all those snorts and giggles?

"Everybody get up and move your desks against the walls. We need to make space here in the middle."

No one did anything at first. It was such a strange request.

"C'mon. We don't have all day."

So we moved our desks. I tipped mine so the pellets spilled onto the floor.

Mr. Crocker grabbed his chair and set it down in front

of his desk. "Make a circle," he said. So we did. "Now sit."

"On the floor?" Caroline asked.

"Yes. Cross your legs and keep your little hands to yourselves."

"What is this?" Ryan asked.

"Show-and-tell," Mr. Crocker said, as if it should be obvious.

"Seriously?"

"This is kindergarten, right?"

It felt like a slap, the way he said it. I hadn't realized till then how angry he was. Even *I* was scared, and I was the victim.

"Today we're going to talk about our little furry friends. Travis, do *you* have a pet?" He said it in a baby voice, like he was speaking to a three-year-old.

"This is stupid," Travis said.

"Is that your dog's name? Stupid?"

"No."

"But you *have* a dog."

"Yes, I have a dog."

"I thought so. Will you pick up his food, please? Somehow it has strayed into my classroom."

Travis didn't move.

"I said, pick it up. *Now!*"

Travis did the only thing he could. He picked up the

pellets and played it for laughs. But he didn't get any. No one wanted to stick out because no one wanted to be next. So he sat back down and dropped the dog food into the well between his legs.

"Thank you, Travis. Now, let's see—*Ryan*! I'm just guessing here, but I'll bet you also have a dog. You don't strike me as a cat or a canary person."

Ryan didn't answer. He just got to his feet, scooped up a handful of dog food, and sat back down again.

"Angelina?" he said. "How about you?"

This was a total shock. I had no doubt that Mr. Crocker, while supposedly grading papers, had been watching the culprits as they built the pyramid of dog food on my desk. He knew who had done it. But never in a million years would I have suspected any of the Fashionistas, and especially not Angelina.

She wasn't a clown. Her thing was being cool and beautiful. She wouldn't do dog food.

And yet.

"I have a cat," Angelina said brightly, running her fingers through her thick mane of honey-gold, salon-highlighted hair and flashing Mr. Crocker her best *Teen Vogue* smile. "Her name is Colette."

"It would be. Is this some of Colette's food we see before us?"

"*Oui*," Angelina said, "*bien sûr.*"

"Then pick it up, *s'il vous plaît.*"

A few jokers giggled over Mr. Crocker's French, but Angelina rose with the grace of a ballerina and picked up her share of the mess without once losing her cool. I watched in awe. I could almost see why Abby wanted to swim in Angelina's exclusive little pond.

Only then did it occur to me that Abby wasn't there. She should have been. I knew for a fact that she was at school. And she was in Mr. Crocker's class.

"*Merci beaucoup,*" Mr. Crocker said. "Jason—dog or cat?"

"My little sister has a dog. His name is Fluffy."

He was trying to be funny, but Mr. Crocker was not amused. "Just pick it up, Jason. You can't blame this on your sister."

Jason gathered up a handful and sat down.

Mr. Crocker scanned the circle. "Now, where is Abigail?"

I couldn't help it. I gasped. My classmates gave me pitying looks.

"Abby went home," Celine said. "She wasn't feeling well."

"Really? She seemed just fine ten minutes ago."

Celine shrugged.

I got up, grabbed my backpack, and walked out of the room.

I didn't ask to be excused.

I didn't go by the office to sign out.

I didn't tell anyone I was leaving.

I just went.

7

Fake Apologies

MY MOTHER WASN'T HOME WHEN I got back to the apartment. She was up at the publisher's office with Jackson Sloan, working on the Camrath papers. This wasn't something I'd considered when I left school early. But at least I had a just-in-case key safety-pinned to the inside of my backpack. It was the first time I'd ever had to use it.

The minute I walked in, the house phone rang. I let the machine take the call. Not surprisingly, it was the principal, Mrs. Chaffee. She sounded amazingly calm as she left her message.

The next thing Mrs. Chaffee did was call my mother's

cell. I knew this because, not long after, the phone rang again. This time it was Mom. When once again I chose not to answer, she left such a scorching message that I ran over and picked up midsentence.

"I'm here," I said. "I'm fine."

Half an hour later, she was home.

"Sit," she said in her serious voice. "We need to talk." She didn't seem angry, just really upset. That, at least, was a relief.

"Mrs. Chaffee told me what happened at school. But I suspect there's a whole lot more. Joplin, I want you to tell me everything." As she said it, she reached over and tucked a strand of hair behind my ear. I don't think she actually cared about my grooming. She just wanted to touch me. And for some reason, that just did me in. I completely fell apart.

"Oh, baby," she said. "I'm so sorry!"

But I wasn't crying about what had happened at school. Not even about Abby. I was crying because I had my mother back. If only for a moment, she was talking to me, thinking about me, and caring about my feelings. I just sat there sobbing in her arms. I only let go when the hugging and weeping had started to get embarrassing.

After I'd washed my face with cold water and blown my nose about a hundred times, I launched into the whole gruesome story. My mom was already shocked by what she'd heard so far, but when I came to the part about Abby, she gasped and pressed a hand to her heart, like she was literally wounded.

Abby had been a part of our family since I was four years old. And though Mom knew our friendship was over, I hadn't told her about the "bomb" or any of the things Abby had said. Now that I was spilling my guts, it all came out.

"That is so *wrong*," Mom said, drooping back into her chair.

"We're a mean species," I said.

"No, sweetie. Not all of us. Just some."

"I can't go back there."

She nodded. "Not for a while anyway. You need to take a few days off, wait for the dust to settle."

"What kind of dust?"

"You know—the school's response. Calling the parents, suspending the kids, questioning the teachers, setting new rules, a lot of general soul-searching."

"Oh," I said, thrilled to miss it.

And for a very short time I comforted myself with the fairy-tale notion that it'd all be over before I went back to school. Then everything would go back to normal.

Unfortunately, Mrs. Chaffee—meaning well, I'm sure—had come down hard on the five perps, aka the five suspended students. They would be allowed to return to St. Mark's only if they phoned me and apologized. A parent had to supervise the call. And they had to speak to me in person. Leaving a message or sending an email wasn't okay.

Even Mr. Crocker had to apologize. In fact, he was the first. He said he'd handled the situation badly. He'd allowed his anger to direct his behavior and failed to consider how his little exercise was going to make me feel. He took full responsibility for what must have been a terribly difficult moment for me, and *blah-blah-blah*.

I didn't *want* to have that conversation with Mr. Crocker. And I definitely didn't want to talk to the others, to listen to their fake apologies and give them my fake forgiveness.

But they had no choice, and neither did I.

The calls came in like clockwork, between five and six that evening. Mrs. Chaffee must have given them a schedule.

I think Mr. Crocker was genuinely sincere. But he was the only one. The boys—Travis, Jason, and Ryan— seemed sort of confused. They really couldn't understand why everybody was making such a huge deal about a stupid little joke. And they totally couldn't believe the consequences. *Suspension?* You'd think they'd committed murder or something!

They didn't say any of this, of course. Not with their parents looming over them. But I could hear it in their voices.

Angelina was a whole other story. She wasn't any sorrier than the boys, but not for the same reason. She knew perfectly well that what they'd done was way out of line. She just didn't think the rules applied to her. Because she was special.

She worded her apology so cleverly that the call was over before I realized what she'd actually said. She'd made it all about *me* and how *I'd* responded to the prank. She'd said, "I'm sorry you were so upset by what we did." In other words, she was "sorry" I couldn't take a joke. Using the word *upset* instead of *hurt* was pure genius.

Say what you will about Angelina, but she is really smart.

The call from Abby came last, and it was thumbscrews all the way. She started out in this squeaky, breathless, little-girl voice, like she was being squeezed by a giant anaconda. Then she progressed to sobbing and gulping out words. She kept saying, over and over, "I didn't want to! I didn't want to do it!"

"Well, who made you, then?" I snapped back.

But as soon as I said it, I knew. *Angelina* had made her do it. That was the price of admission to the inner circle.

Of course Abby couldn't answer my question because she was crying too hard. And I really couldn't bear another second of her hysteria.

"It's all right," I said. "I forgive you."

Then I hung up the phone.

All this time, Mom had sat beside me, holding my hand. It felt so good I almost wished there were going to be more calls, just so we could stay together like that.

But there weren't and we didn't.

"There, that's done," she said. "Now it's over." She gave my hand one last squeeze, then went into the kitchen to start dinner.

The next morning Mom left early for her conference with Mrs. Chaffee. She assured me that I'd be safe. There were agents watching our apartment and she'd be back as soon as the meeting was over.

She'd always been like that—crazy overprotective, like she thought I might disappear if I was left alone for five minutes. And so it didn't surprise me at all that, except for the meeting at school, she stayed home all three days.

But she might as well have been on Mars for all the good it did me. She was always in her room with the door shut, banging away on her father's antique Royal Quiet DeLuxe. I asked her why she was using an ancient manual typewriter when she owned a perfectly good—and genuinely quiet—laptop computer. She said she wanted to know "how it felt."

I can tell you how *I* felt, and it wasn't good.

My brief, heady moment of parental attention was clearly over. It was like she'd turned into a zombie, like all her feelings and spirit had been sucked right out of her, leaving her empty inside. Or rather, she still had feelings—but just the sad ones.

By the time Thursday rolled around, it was a real toss-up as to which was worse—staying home with Mom or going back to school.

Our plan had always been for me to go back on Friday. The perps would be suspended till Monday, so they wouldn't be there. And I'd have the weekend to recover from the reentry. I'd agreed that this made sense, but I definitely wasn't looking forward to it.

That night Jen came home early carrying a bulky package in a large canvas bag.

"Is that my platter?" I asked.

"It is indeed. And wait till you see. Lucius Doyle himself couldn't have done a better job."

She set the package carefully on the kitchen table, got some scissors out of a drawer, and went to work on the tape that fastened the cardboard supports and the swaddling of Bubble Wrap. It took a while and made a mess, but finally there it was—my platter, in all its glory, lying in a nest of plastic wrapping.

It didn't look like an old broken thing that had been glued back together. It looked like a work of art. The pond, the sweet little girl driving her geese to water, and behind them the trees and the clouds overhead, and a tiny windmill off in the distance—all of it felt amazingly real. To look at that scene was like traveling back to a faraway place in some long-ago time, before America was even a country.

Mom stood back, like she couldn't allow herself to be happy or excited about anything. But curiosity finally got the best of her. She came over and had a look.

"Well," she said after a long silence. "That certainly is a beautiful thing. I'm glad you saved it, Joplin. I was just a little kid when it was broken. I guess I never looked at it properly. It's wonderful."

"Didn't Mrs. Berenson do a splendid job?" Jen was very proud of herself.

"Yes, yes!" I said, giving her a big squeeze. "Thank you, thank you, thank you!"

"Wait!" Jen said. "There's more!"

She reached into the canvas bag and pulled out something else. It was also wrapped in cardboard and plastic, only this was the kind of packaging you get when you buy stuff in stores.

"Ta-da! A plate-hanger thingie! Just the perfect size."

"Can we hang it over my bed?"

"Of course."

"Right now?"

"Why not?"

8

Wishes

I WAS READING *Anne of Green Gables* for the second time. I'd picked that particular book because I already knew I liked it. I hoped it would calm me down and help me get to sleep.

But I'd forgotten all about Diana Barry, Anne Shirley's "bosom friend."

I'd been in third grade the first time I read it. And, as Ms. Warrick would say, it totally rocked my world. I wanted to *be* Anne Shirley. I wanted to live on Prince Edward Island. I think I sort of even wanted to be an orphan—no offense to my very nice parents, of course. For a while I wore my hair in braids, though it wasn't really long enough (and worse, it wasn't red like Anne's).

Then one day a fifth grader, whose locker was across from mine, had asked if I was the kid who always hung out with Abby Strasser. I guess she was interested because Abby's dad is this big Broadway producer and pretty famous.

I said, "Yes, she's my bosom friend."

Well, it was awful. I didn't realize, till I saw the expression on the girl's face, just how totally stupid that sounded. By the time the bell rang at the end of the day, it was all over the school. I was marked forever as the weird kid who said *bosom*.

So, reading the book I used to love now made me unspeakably sad. Not only did it remind me of a horribly embarrassing moment; it also reminded me that, unlike Anne Shirley (and the third-grade Joplin Danforth), I no longer had a bosom friend.

Not even a non-bosom, run-of-the-mill, say-hi-in-the-hall kind of friend.

I had nobody. No one. Nada.

I got up, grabbed a Kleenex, and blew my nose. Then I stood by my bed and looked at my platter, carefully hung by Jen.

It was such a restful scene. A little like I imagined Prince Edward Island to be—pretty countryside, not too many people. The girl by the pond certainly looked happy, and *she* didn't have a friend.

She had geese, though.

I thought, *Maybe I should get a dog.*

"I'll bet *you* never had to go to school," I said to the girl by the pond.

Then it struck me that not going to school wasn't really such a wonderful thing. Girls back then didn't have a choice. They probably just stayed home and worked all the time, doing whatever their parents said—until they were married off at, like, fourteen or fifteen, after which they would have to do whatever their *husband* said. And it would go on like that, just work and more work, plus having tons of babies to take care of, until they died too young of something we could easily cure today.

It made me remember how lucky I was, which lifted the gloom a little.

I knelt on my bed and studied the girl up close. She wasn't just decoration, like the windmill and the geese. She looked like a real person. She seemed sweet and maybe kind of shy, used to being by herself a lot, taking care of the animals and doing chores.

I wondered if she was lonely too.

"I wish you could be my friend," I whispered. "Then at least we'd have each other."

I really do wonder about myself sometimes. How, in a mere six seconds, had I managed to make a U-turn from feeling lucky to wallowing in my loneliness again? I wasn't *trying* to be miserable. I didn't *enjoy* it. But being upbeat and positive wasn't going to change the facts. I had become a person nobody liked.

Worse, I now had a big old bull's-eye painted on my back. Making fun of Joplin had become the hot new form of entertainment. True, things would die down for a while, because being suspended was a drag. But nothing would really change. I'd still be an outcast. If anything, the perps would blame me for "getting them in trouble," and . . .

Oh, stop it! I told myself, and turned off the light.

Not that I was likely to get much sleep with all those bad thoughts having a riot in my head. But I'd better try, since I had to get up and go to school in the morning. So I pulled out one of my regular sleep-inducing exercises and added extra complexities to it. That way, I'd have to concentrate harder, and the bad thoughts would quiet down.

I decided to list first *and* last names that began with sequential letters, alternating genders. Extra points for real people.

Alice Bates.

Charlie Davis.

Ellen Frasier.

George Harrison. (Extra point.)

Ida Jones.

Any of you want to be my friend?

Karl Lancaster.

Maria Nuñez.

Seriously—no takers? Not even one? I just wish I had one friend, preferably someone who goes to my school. Is that really asking too much?

Oliver Pickle . . .

The next morning I woke feeling awful. I hadn't slept nearly enough. Now I was ragged and almost sick. Mom and Jen were already in the kitchen. I could hear their voices and the clatter of dishes.

I went to the bathroom to get ready. When I'd finished washing my face, I stared at myself in the mirror, trying to picture how I must look to other people.

Ordinary, I decided. Average. Plain. Maybe I should let my hair grow long and buy a curling iron.

Young, at least compared to the Fashionistas. They looked fifteen; I looked ten.

Serious and smart. That is to say, nerdy. But mostly it was my expression that made me look that way. Maybe if I smiled more, people would like me better. I tried one of Angelina's *Teen Vogue* smiles. The result was not good.

I searched my closet for something to wear that might improve my image but didn't have much luck. I laid three combos out on the bed, but there wasn't a winner in the bunch. They all looked like me.

Just then, out of the corner of my eye, I noticed something unexpected in the garden.

Something that wasn't green or brown.

I went to the window and looked out.

Sitting on the bench beside the fountain was a girl about my age.

In all the years we'd lived in our apartment, I'd never seen another child out there (except for the little screamers with their nannies, but they didn't count).

Maybe a new family had moved into one of the brownstones. With a girl my age who liked gardens. How amazing was that?

I dressed in a rush, no longer caring what I wore, and hollered to Jen to ask if I could go through her room to the garden.

Jen called back, "Sure!"

Mom added, "Make it snappy!"

I said I would.

When the door opened, the girl turned and smiled at me. I went over and sat beside her on the bench.

At a glance I noticed how pretty she was. Angelina would die for that beautiful skin, not to mention the natural blond hair. If the girl did something with it, besides wearing it in braids, she could be a Fashionista.

But judging by her dress, I had the feeling she wouldn't want to. It was plain blue cotton and looked suspiciously like her mother had run it up on the sewing machine. There was something white folded up beside her, tucked under her skirt. I couldn't tell what it was. Probably a collar or a jacket, which her clueless mom thought was absolutely adorable but the girl knew would be the last nail in her coffin, fashion-wise. So she'd taken it off.

"Hi," I said. "I'm Joplin—after Scott Joplin, the ragtime composer, and Janis Joplin, the rock singer. There's also a Joplin, Missouri, but I'm not named after that."

The girl blinked, confused. Too much information, I guess. I do tend to run off at the mouth whenever I get nervous.

"I live over there," I added, pointing. "At number twenty-three."

When she just stared at our back door, I decided I

should ask questions instead of telling her stuff. That way she'd *have* to talk.

"Are you new here?" I tried.

"Yes," she said.

"What's your name?"

She hesitated for a couple of beats, which struck me as kind of weird. "Sofie," she finally said.

"Do you live near here?" I made a circle with my finger, taking in the backs of the brownstones that walled in the garden.

"Yes," she said again.

Maybe she was just super shy, but I couldn't seem to get the conversation going. Also, I was starting to worry because Mom would be mad if I stayed out here too long. But I was afraid to leave for fear I'd never see Sofie again. I just knew that once she opened up, she'd be my new bosom friend.

"Listen, Sofie," I said, "I have to go get ready for school. But if you want to hang out or something this afternoon"— oh, cheez, that sounded so lame!—"I'll meet you here."

"All right," Sofie said. She was grinning, so I figured she really meant it.

We said good-bye and I hurried back inside, careful to lock the door so I wouldn't get fussed at, and joined Mom and Jen for breakfast.

"You look cheery this morning," Mom said, sounding pleasantly surprised.

I shrugged. We all knew how I felt about going back to school.

I could see that Mom was just dying to give me all sorts of annoying advice but sensed that it would only stir things up. Jen sensed it too and changed the subject.

"I asked one of my colleagues at work if he'd ever heard of Hans van der Brock. He said no, but he'd do some research. I'll ask him again today."

"Thanks, Jen. You do nice things."

Jen beamed. Mom did too. I was exceeding all their expectations. I deserved at least three gold stars.

And the truth was, I did feel a bit more hopeful. Whatever happened at school, I'd have Sofie waiting when I got home. And there was the chance—maybe a really small one, but a chance just the same—that she'd turn out to be the friend that Abby used to be.

I went to my room to get my backpack. Also to make sure Sofie was still in the garden.

That was affirmative. I waved at her and she waved back.

Then I turned to say a brief good-bye to my very own original seventeenth-century masterpiece by the mysterious Hans van der Brock—and froze. It was like an electric current had passed through my body and stopped my heart.

The scene was the same as before: pond, geese, grass, trees, clouds, windmill.

But the girl was gone.

9

The Boy with
All the Hair

"YOU ALL RIGHT?" JEN GAVE me this searching look when I came back into the kitchen. It must have been all over my face.

"Just nervous." My voice sounded strange—breathy, like I couldn't quite push the words out.

"Joplin—" Mom started in. But I didn't let her finish.

"Gotta go," I said, grabbing my lunch off the counter, stuffing it into my backpack, and hurrying out the door. Once I was safely outside, I stopped on the sidewalk to get my breathing under control.

A small clump of die-hard photographers were loitering

across the street. I glared over, daring them to take so much as a step in my direction. They didn't move an inch, and somehow that little triumph tamped down my panic just a smidge. I headed off to school, walking fast.

I'd already reached some really freakish conclusions about my new neighbor. But I needed time to absorb and consider them. The trick was to keep my head from exploding in the process—which, let me tell you, wasn't easy.

On the one hand, it seemed really obvious: The girl had disappeared from my platter and a girl who looked just like her suddenly appeared in our garden. They had to be the same.

But that worked only if I threw scientific logic and a lifetime of experience right out the window. Girls didn't come and go from platters. They just didn't.

And yet, how else to explain what I saw?

So it went, round and round.

Needless to say, I didn't learn a thing at school that day. And maybe the fact that I was so distracted is the reason my reentry went as smoothly as it did. The other kids—not the perps, who weren't there, but the rest of them, the ones who'd just sat there while the whole thing went down, who hadn't tried to help, who maybe even thought it was kind of funny—well, they left me alone.

They could tell that my mind was somewhere very far away, certainly not on them. And they were probably sick to death of the Joplin Danforth saga anyway.

So they were polite, they didn't stare, and I went back to being invisible. Meanwhile, inside my head, it was like an old-fashioned pinball machine, thoughts pinging off each other, flying in every direction. But no one seemed to notice how worried and distracted I was. Or, if they did, they thought they knew the reason why.

As usual, I went to the library for lunch and Ms. Finney smiled when I came in. Also as usual, I took my regular seat at the far right corner table, artfully placing my backpack to act as a shield, and taking out my brown-bag lunch.

Not quite as usual, Ms. Finney waited a discreet amount of time, then came over and sat beside me.

Silently, my spirit groaned.

"I've been thinking," Ms. Finney said, once again blind to all evidence of illegal food consumption in the library.

"What about?" I said, swallowing with a gulp.

"There's somebody I think you need to know. He's older than you, in sixth grade, but you're mature for your age. And you have a lot in common. I think you'd get on like a house afire."

I blinked. That was so unexpected.

"Mind if I play matchmaker?" I just gaped at her, so she kept on trying. "He's the Sherlock Holmes fan, remember?"

Of course I did. The boy with all the hair. He was adorable.

"He's still waiting for *The Hound of the Baskervilles*. Maybe if you offered to lend him your copy, it would break the ice."

Is she trying to set us up on a date?

"C'mon, Joplin. Live large. Take a chance."

Since things couldn't possibly get any weirder, I said, "Sure."

Moments later she was back with my date.

He was way tall, even for a sixth grader. I bet people were always asking him if he played basketball. And he had a really nice face under all those dorky curls.

"Joplin Danforth, this is Barrett Browning. Barrett, Joplin has a full set of Sherlock Holmes. If you're really nice to her, she might lend it to you."

Barrett seemed thrilled to hear this. "Have you read them all?" he asked, taking a seat across from me, folding his arms, and settling in like we were old friends.

I said, "Yes, I have." I said, "Sherlock Holmes is awesome." I said, "I'll be glad to bring the set to school on Monday."

The ice, as Ms. Finney put it, was broken and melting fast.

I hadn't felt such an instant connection since meeting Abby at the Presbyterian church preschool. I couldn't remember the actual moment. I was, after all, only four at the time. But I do remember how we both liked building castles with oversize Legos. We spent way more time in the science-and-discovery section than any of the other kids. And we were the first to learn how to write our names. Right from the start it had felt like we belonged together.

It was the same with Barrett Browning now, only better. It was easy to talk to him. I could just be myself and not worry that he would think I was weird.

I bet I could even have said "bosom friend" and he wouldn't have turned a hair.

Since we'd started with Sherlock, we talked about books for a while. He'd read different ones than I had, but they were the same *kind* of books, mostly old, like *Anne of Green Gables* or *The Count of Monte Cristo*. And mostly they hadn't been written for kids. I guess you'd call them "classics." I made a list of his favorites. I knew I'd like them.

I told him that my aunt Jen—who wasn't actually my aunt—had majored in art history in college and worked at Christie's, which was a big auction house for art, so she knew all about it. Sometimes she took me to the Met Museum and gave me a personal tour.

Most kids, if I told them that, would give me a blank stare or roll their eyes. But Barrett thought it was cool. He liked the Met too. His favorite part was the Egyptian section, especially the wooden models of boats and houses. He said that at first glance they weren't nearly as impressive as the mummies and temples. But he liked them best because they showed the everyday lives of ancient Egyptians, not just the pharaohs. Also, wasn't it amazing that wooden models could have survived for *five thousand years*?

I said yes, it was totally amazing. Jen said it was because the land in Egypt was so dry that the wood didn't rot.

Then Barrett told me about this three-thousand-year-old mummy of a temple singer from Luxor, and how they did a CAT scan on it, then used this special software, made for designing cars, to turn the data into 3D images of her body. Now they were planning to digitally re-create her singing voice.

While he was telling me all this, another electrical surge ran through me, and once again it felt like my heart had quit beating. I made a strange choking sound. Barrett stopped talking and stared at me.

"Barrett," I said, "can you keep a secret?"

He sat up a little straighter. "Sure."

My heart was beating again, only now it was pounding and I could hardly breathe. At the same time, I felt this sudden wave of relief: *There was someone I could tell!*

"You'll think I'm making this up, but I promise I'm not."

"All right." I loved his expression. He was interested, waiting, serious. His mind was wide open.

"There's this old Dutch platter. Really old, like from the 1600s. It belonged to my grandparents, but it was broken years ago, back when my mom was little. After my grandfather died, I found the pieces in an old cookie tin. My mom said I could have it. And my aunt Jen found an expert to glue the pieces back together."

Barrett listened patiently.

"It's beautiful, a scene in the country with a pond and trees and a windmill and stuff. And by the pond is a girl and some geese."

"I can picture it."

The bell rang. We ignored it.

"So we hung it on the wall over my bed." I took a deep breath. "Then last night I was lying there, feeling kind of sad and lonely. I started thinking about the girl in the picture and thought she looked lonely too. I wished she could be my friend. And then later, while I was trying to get to sleep, I wished I had a friend at school."

I paused. Barrett was on high alert, excitement all over his face. "Let me guess," he said. "I'm the one at school."

I nodded, amazed that he got it so fast. "Yes, I think you are."

"And the girl?"

"She was in the garden this morning."

He gasped. "You're giving me chills! I think I know what you're going to say next."

"You probably do. I looked at the platter before I left . . ."

"And she was gone."

"Yes!"

He sucked in a huge breath and let it out with a long "*Woooowwww!*"

"I feel like maybe I'm losing my mind."

"Yeah, I can imagine! Okay, let me think. What if I went home with you this afternoon to borrow the Sherlock Holmes? I could look at the platter and, you know, maybe see the girl in the garden?"

"Oh, would you please?"

"Are you kidding me? I wouldn't miss this for the world."

10

The F-Word

Mom was in her room as usual, typing away. I knocked on her door.

"What is it, Joplin?"

She sounded snappish, which made me want to snap back. So I opened the door without asking permission.

She looked up, her face set in annoyance. Then it changed to surprise when she saw this very tall, unfamiliar boy standing right behind me.

"Mom, this is my friend, Barrett Browning."

I figured the f-word would give her a charge. Apparently it did. She sprang out of her chair like she'd sat on a cat. I could practically read her thoughts: *Joplin has a friend?*

"Hello, Barrett," she said. Big, warm smile.

"In case you're wondering," I explained, "he isn't related to Elizabeth Barrett Browning, because actually she was Elizabeth Barrett before she married Robert Browning, so technically Barrett Browning is a combo of the two—"

"Got it, Joplin." She was smiling the way parents do when their kids say something silly but cute, like "I'm not *really* a monster, Mommy. Don't be scared!"

It was kind of embarrassing.

"Anyway, since his mother is a poet and their name is Browning, she couldn't resist."

Mom nodded, looking at Barrett. "I like names that come with stories."

"Also," Barrett added, "my mom liked the alliteration."

The gears in her brain were turning even faster now: *What a smart kid, just the right amount of geekiness. They're a perfect match.*

"Can Barrett borrow our set of Sherlock Holmes? He wants to read *The Hound of the Baskervilles* but the library copy's checked out."

"Of course he can."

"Thanks," Barrett said. "I'll take good care of it, I promise. And I hope you don't mind, but I couldn't help noticing your typewriter. It looks seriously vintage."

"It is. It belonged to my father."

"You mean—*Martin J. Camrath*?"

"Yes."

"That is *so awesome*!"

"She's writing a mystery," I said. "But she publishes under a pseudonym, Millicent Clark, because she doesn't want her father's fame to define her."

At this point Mom laughed out loud. "Actually, Barrett, I've put the mystery aside. I'm working on a memoir now."

"On Martin J. Camrath's typewriter?" Barrett said. "That is so extremely cool!"

"Yes, well, it's only an exercise for now. I'm afraid it's not very good."

I was starting to feel anxious, worried that Sofie might not be there. So I nudged Barrett gently away from the door.

"We won't bother you anymore, Mrs. Danforth," he said. "But it was a tremendous pleasure to meet you."

I closed the door.

"I just saw Martin J. Camrath's typewriter!"

"I know," I said. "Get over it. Come on."

I led him into my room, raced to the window, and heaved a sigh of relief. Sofie was still there, sitting on the same bench where I'd left her that morning. It was as if she hadn't moved at all.

"Is that her?"

"Yes," I said. "But first let me show you this." We stood in front of the platter and I touched the place by the pond, empty now. "She was right there," I said. "Beside the geese."

Barrett was leaning in, squinting as he studied every detail. "It's like she was on a different layer—you know, the way they do in animation? The background was on one layer and she was on another. That's why there isn't a bare space where she used to be. She was transported out of the platter, but everything else stayed the same."

"*Transported?*"

"I don't know what to call it. Sounds right."

"Want to meet her?"

"What do you think?"

"This way."

Sofie looked up when she heard the door open, same as before. This time she got to her feet and smiled.

"Sofie, this is my friend, Barrett."

That was the second time I'd used the f-word in the last ten minutes. It was starting to feel normal.

"Hi," she said, and reached out her hand.

Barrett's face flushed, and for a nanosecond he seemed to freeze. I couldn't tell if he was afraid to touch her because maybe she was a ghost or whether he'd noticed her sea-blue eyes, glossy blond hair, and creamy complexion and was feeling a little weak in the knees.

Whatever it was, he got over it pretty quickly. He took her hand in this formal, old-fashioned way, like some heroine's elderly father out of a 1930s movie.

"Have you been waiting here all this time?" I asked.

"Yes," Sofie said. "I didn't mind. But I should tell you that a man came over and spoke to me this morning. He was concerned that I was sitting so close to your door. He asked me a lot of questions, like whether I lived in one of these . . ." She indicated the brownstones that circled the garden, as if she couldn't find the right word.

"Apartments?"

"Yes, apartments. I told him I was your friend and I was waiting for you. He's watching us now, from over by the church. Maybe he won't be so worried, now that he's seen us together. But if you'd like for me to wait somewhere else . . ."

"Wait—hold on! Are you saying that you *don't have any place to go?* I mean, don't you *live* somewhere?"

"I live here."

"In the *garden*?"

"Well, it seemed better than suddenly appearing in your room. I didn't want to frighten you."

I just stood there and stared. I could feel the blood pulsing through my arteries. I felt light in the head, like I was going to faint. "Are you here just for *me*?"

"Yes."

"Because I wished you could be my friend?"

She nodded.

"And Barrett? Did you have anything to do with him?"

She was blinking back tears now. "I'm sorry if I made a mistake. You said you wanted a friend at school."

I was momentarily speechless. Barrett's mouth was open, like he was getting ready to say something, so I put a hand on his arm to stop him. An important thought was trying to form in my mind and I didn't want to lose it.

"Sofie, I didn't *say* I wanted a friend at school. I *thought* it. Silently. In my mind."

"Well, it's sort of the same thing." Her voice was perfectly calm.

"Does that mean you can *hear my thoughts*?"

"If you want me to leave, you have only to wish it."

That was too much. "I need to sit down," I said.

I must have gone pale because Barrett took me by the arm, and since there wasn't room on the bench for three, he led me over to a plot of grass. "We can sit here," he said, guiding me gently as I stepped over the boxwood border. He didn't let go till I was safely seated. He waved Sofie over to join us and we sat in a circle.

"Okay," I said, still breathing hard, still feeling my whole body on high alert, "can you hear what I'm thinking now?" I looked down at my hands and forced myself to focus: *Atlanta, Boston, Chicago, Dallas, East Lansing, Fredonia—*

"No."

"But you said . . ."

"It's confusing for me too," Sofie said. "And I don't exactly know how it works, except that when you wish something, I become aware of it."

"Why?"

"Because you own the platter. And"—she looked embarrassed, as if what she was about to say was indelicate and embarrassing—"I guess that means you own me too. I am compelled to give you anything you wish for."

I didn't know how to respond to that. For a moment

I simply sat there, openmouthed with astonishment over what had just been said.

That's when it came to me, loud and clear, that reality as I'd known it was only part of a much bigger picture. There were other realities that followed different rules—and we had just entered one of them. Barrett, Sofie, and I had just passed through the wardrobe into our own personal Narnia.

"Are you all right?" Sofie asked.

"Yeah. Sort of. Making some mental adjustments, that's all."

She nodded. She understood.

I noticed again the little bundle of white cloth. Sofie had carried it with her when she left the bench and had tucked it under her skirt as we sat on the grass.

"What is that?" I asked, though I was pretty sure I already knew.

"My clothes."

"Your apron and your little cap?"

"Yes. I took them off because I was afraid they would look peculiar. It's not how people dress now."

"May I see?"

She pulled out the bundle and handed it to me. I studied the cap, with its carefully hand-stitched edge. "Did you make this?"

"My mother did."

Barrett leaned over to see. I handed it to him, watched as he studied the shape of it, the way it folded back and hung down at the sides.

"Where is she now?" I asked. "Your mother."

Sofie flinched, but she answered. "That was long ago," she said. "She's gone. I have no mother now."

Of course. Her mother would have lived in the 1600s. And all this time since then, for hundreds of years . . .

"Joplin," Barrett said, handing the cap back to Sofie. "Do you mind if I ask her a question? I think it's important."

I nodded.

"Sofie—*before* last night, when Joplin wished you were her friend, what was it like for you? Being a picture on a platter, I mean." It sounded so bold for him to say it out loud like that.

"I was looking out at Joplin and the room. I have always looked out at whatever place I was."

"And before that? When the platter was broken? What was it like then?"

"Nothing," Sofie said. "Just darkness and forgetting. Like a dreamless sleep."

Like death. I shuddered.

Barrett leaned over and covered his face with his hands,

then ran his fingers through his hair, clutching at his head like it was in danger of falling off. "Sofie, can you tell us *what you are?*"

"I am a person."

"An actual flesh-and-blood person?" Barrett asked. "You need to eat, and sleep, and . . . all the rest? Do you feel pain?"

"Yes. I am like any person."

"But you're not. You—"

"Barrett, wait!" I said. "Sofie, if what you say is true—"

She nodded.

"—and you've been sitting here since last night, you must be starving."

"I *am* hungry," she admitted.

I got to my feet on trembling legs, using Barrett's shoulder for balance. "You eat regular food?"

"Yes."

"Then I'm going to go make you a sandwich. Do you need to use the bathroom?"

She blushed. Of course she did. She was like any other person.

We slipped quietly into the house. I showed Sofie where to go, left Barrett standing watch at the door, and went in the kitchen to make her a sandwich. While I was spreading mayo and mustard on bread and piling on the ham and cheese, I was trying to think in a logical way about something that defied logic so completely as to be totally unbelievable.

Yet there Sofie was, in the flesh, using our bathroom.

The first and most obvious question I faced was: Should I tell my mom?

I wanted to, desperately. But my instincts said no. She'd been weird ever since our week in Maine, off in her own private world, thinking dark thoughts and on the verge of tears most of the time.

Jen kept saying she was "fragile right now" and begging me "not to make things worse." Telling her that the girl in the platter had come alive and was living in our garden—well, that probably *would* make things worse.

But there was something else, something even more important. If my mom knew that Sofie had no place to live, she'd call child services or whatever you call it. They'd take her away and put her in a foster home.

That's not what I wanted. I doubted Sofie wanted it either. She'd appeared for only one reason: to be my friend. I understood that it hadn't been her choice. She had to obey my wishes because the platter belonged to me. But that no longer mattered. She *felt* like my friend, and I wanted to help.

So before we told anybody anything, Barrett and I needed to figure things out.

I looked in the fridge for something to go with the sandwich and found a couple of tangerines. Then I got a snack-size bag of potato chips from the cupboard, put everything in a lunch bag, and went back to the fridge for a bottle of water.

Done.

But that was just one meal. And if Sofie really was a "regular person" (when not living in a delftware platter), then she'd need three meals a day. She'd need shelter from the weather, a place to sleep, the use of a bathroom, and clothes to wear.

She was, by definition, a homeless person.

And she was my responsibility.

11

Someplace to Live

"We believe this, right?" I whispered to Barrett, who was standing guard at our bathroom door. Inside, water was running in the sink.

"I think we have to."

"It's not a hallucination?"

"She seems pretty real to me."

"Yeah, she does."

The door opened and Sofie peeked cautiously out. And suddenly all my doubts were washed away.

"Come on," I said, taking her hand and leading her

through Jen's empty room and out the back door, Barrett following close behind. "We need to talk."

We sat in our circle on the grass while Sofie ate her sandwich. As I watched, I couldn't stop thinking of all those hours she'd spent in the garden with nothing to eat or drink. All night, alone, as one by one the lights went out in the apartments around her. Listening as the sounds of traffic gradually faded away, until it was dark and quiet—or as dark and quiet as it ever gets in New York—and more than a little bit scary.

Did she lie down on the bench to sleep? She must have, though it wasn't really long enough. Her legs would have dangled off the end. She must have been stiff and cold from lying on that hard stone slab with no blanket or pillow.

And then, come morning, I'd appeared, but just for a minute and totally clueless. That was followed by six or seven more hours of tedium, the sun beating down on her head and back while she sat there waiting, waiting, waiting—hungry, thirsty, bored, and sad.

It made me sick to imagine those things.

"Sofie," I said, "this is all my fault. I'm so sorry."

She shook her head, gulping down a mouthful of sandwich.

"No!" she said. "I'm glad. I would much rather be a person than the way I was. I can speak, and feel things, and talk with other people after all those years of just looking out at the world."

I pictured that too—hanging from a wall or propped on a shelf, watching people come and go, hearing their conversations, but mostly just staring at the same scene for hours, days, years. "It must have been awful," I said.

"Yes. But I used the time well. I learned English by listening to conversations. I learned about people too. They're so different, you know, one from the other. And more complicated than I ever could have imagined before I saw so many lives unfold.

"And then, when things were quiet—the nights and often the days as well—I spoke to myself in Dutch so I wouldn't lose the language. I thought about my family, so I wouldn't forget them. But I do sometimes wonder whether I actually remember *them* or just the facts I kept telling myself over and over."

"Sofie," I said, seeing Barrett ready to jump in and start asking a million questions, the same questions I wanted to ask. "We really, really want to hear your story. And even more than that, we want to figure out how we can help you. But before we do anything, we need to find you a place to live. You can't stay here in the garden. It gets cold, and it rains, and people will notice. You need food and shelter and a place to sleep."

She nodded, peeling a tangerine with practiced hands, as though she'd done it before.

"The obvious thing would be for you to live with me. But then I'd have to explain you to my mother, and that would cause all kinds of problems. More than you can imagine."

"I understand about the problems."

"Right," I said, taking a deep breath. "Now, the good news is that this is a Friday. There's no school on Saturday or Sunday, so I'll be here all day."

She was eating again, but she nodded to say that she understood.

"I'll introduce you to my mom as a new friend. I'll say I've invited you to spend the weekend. That'll give us a couple of days to come up with something."

She nodded again, swallowed, then studied the plastic cap on the water bottle, perplexed. Barrett took it from her and twisted off the top. "Like that," he said, handing it back. Sofie took a long, deep drink, then heaved a little sigh of relief.

"I'll come over in the morning," Barrett said. "Then maybe we could take a picnic up to Central Park—sit there and talk in private. Does that sound like fun?" He was looking at Sofie, not at me.

"Whatever Joplin wants," she said.

"I'll tell you what Joplin wants," I said. "I want you to act like a regular person, not a genie out of a lamp who has to grant my wishes. Just be my friend, okay? Can you do that?"

"Yes," she says. "I've done it before."

I blinked. "You have?"

"I was a person once before. For eleven years."

"Long ago?"

"Sort of. Not too long. I'm not entirely sure."

"Good. That means you know how things work."

She nodded.

"And that makes things easier—because I've actually sort of come up with an idea. It's not perfect, maybe just a temporary solution, but it's better than nothing. Only you'd have to seem, you know, pretty normal."

"What's the idea?" Barrett asked.

I hesitated. "It would mean trusting another person."

"Just tell us, Joplin."

"Okay. We have this upstairs neighbor. Her name is Chloe. She used to be my babysitter, but she's in college now, so she's officially a grown-up. Her mom and dad are on sabbatical in France for the spring semester. So at the moment it's just Chloe alone in a two-bedroom apartment."

"Aha," Barrett said.

"She's kind of a different person. But she's lots of fun, up for anything. I don't suppose you've ever seen a girl with pink and blue streaks in her hair."

"No," Sofie said. "Is that usual?"

"It's something people sometimes do for fun. They dye their hair weird colors. Anyway, asking if you can stay in her apartment is going to be tricky. I'm not sure how I'm going to explain it. Maybe I'll come up with something."

"Do you trust her?" Barrett asked. "That's the important thing."

"Yeah, I do. Sofie, what do you think? Be honest."

She put her sandwich down and thought about it. "Well, I don't know her, of course. But you do, and you seem convinced it would work. I can't go on living in the garden, as you said."

"Barrett?"

"I agree. We don't have any other options, so we'll have to trust your judgment about Chloe. But I'd like to ask one question first. It's kind of jumping ahead of things, but we need to have a long-range plan before we get bogged down in the details."

Barrett leaned forward, elbows on knees, and looked directly at Sofie.

"Joplin asked you to be honest, to say what you really feel. So here's the big, big question: What do *you* want?"

"How do you mean?"

"Do you want to go back and be a picture on a platter? Do you want to stay here in New York, maybe with a foster or adoptive family to look after you, so you can go to school, then to college, and grow up to be—I don't know—a teacher, or an accountant, or an astronaut?"

She shook her head, no.

"Why not?"

"I can't 'grow up.' I will always be as I am now. Years pass, but I stay the same. It's as though I'm trapped in a moment of time that goes on forever."

"Oh!" I said, shocked. "And you know this from when you were a person before?"

"Yes. It's one of the complications."

"Just for now, forget all that and ask yourself, within the bounds of your reality: If you could do *anything at all*, what would you choose for yourself and your future?"

She didn't hesitate. "I would go home."

"To Holland?"

"Yes. But as I said, that was a long time ago. My family and my home aren't there anymore. There is no going back. It's impossible."

"What if I wished you were back at home?" I said. "Not in Holland as it is now, but at the time when you lived there."

"We tried that. It didn't work. For some reason sending me home is different from other wishes. You don't have the power to do it."

Barrett got up and paced in circles. I figured this was what he did when he was trying to work something out. Finally he sat down again.

"It's like a puzzle," he said. "A really hard puzzle with lots of pieces. But if this is real—and I think it is—then there must be some kind of internal logic to it. We just have to find the answer, and that's going to take time. Meanwhile, you need to be somewhere comfortable and safe."

"All right," I said, getting to my feet. "Let's go do this thing."

12

The Short Version

BACK IN THE OLDEN DAYS, before our building was broken up into four separate apartments, it belonged to a single family. The owners used the top three floors, while the servants lived and worked in the basement, where I now lived with Mom and Jen.

The servants had their own humble entrance, aka our front door, cleverly hidden under the flight of seven wide stone steps that led up to Chloe's stoop and the formal entry door. Which is where we now stood, waiting for her to let us in.

Naturally, the Martinellis' apartment was nicer than

ours. Not as big, since the stairway took space from the top three apartments, but it had fancy moldings, high ceilings, big windows, and wooden floors with a ribbon design around the edge.

You'd think they'd have bought fancy antique furniture to go with the old-fashioned rooms. But the Martinellis were super artsy and into "midcentury modern," which I never quite understood, except that it's stuff that was in style back in the 1950s.

I'd asked Chloe about it once or twice, and I guess I was a little too persistent and also totally clueless, because she finally said, "It's just a *thing*, Joplin—okay?"

Anyway, the place was all shag rugs and bright-colored furniture in these weird, swoopy shapes. "Be prepared," I told Sofie and Barrett. "It's kind of different."

"Like Chloe?"

"Yeah."

Chloe buzzed us in. When we reached her apartment, she was waiting for us, the door already opened. She had on overalls and a sleeveless T-shirt, her hair pulled up with a fat clip. It looked like a multicolored fountain was erupting from her head.

"Hey," she said. "Wazzup? We having a party?"

"Not exactly," I said. "These are just my friends." And I made the introductions.

Chloe seemed highly amused. She probably thought Barrett was my boyfriend.

"Actually, we have a weird question to ask. Kind of a favor."

"Come on in," she said, waving us in the direction of their lime-green, notoriously uncomfortable, apparently stylish sofa. We sat in a row like three little soldiers while Chloe slouched across from us in an orange molded chair.

"So what's the weird favor?" she asked. "I can't wait to hear."

"Um," I began, "it's pretty simple, really. My friend Sofie needs someplace to hang for a while. She's not a runaway or anything like that, I promise. It's just that she has this really complicated problem and we're trying to help her with it, but that'll take some time. So I thought maybe she . . ."

"Could stay here?"

"Yeah, basically that's it."

"Just curious, but since she's your friend, wouldn't she rather live with you?"

"Well, that's the problem. See, I can't tell Mom about her situation. It's complicated."

"So you've already mentioned."

Chloe stared up in the general direction of the ceiling, took out the clip, and started playing with her hair—pulling it back like she was making a ponytail, twisting it in a knot, then letting it go again. She did this over and over, just staring into space and not saying a word.

I looked over at Sofie. She was sitting very stiff and straight, like a little kid on her best behavior, hands in her lap. I suddenly had this really bad feeling that Chloe was winding herself up to say no. And I didn't have a second option. This was my one and only idea.

"I'm cool with Sofie staying here," she finally said. "But I'm not getting in the middle of some weird family situation."

"There is no weird family situation."

"Bad custody decision? Foster family gone terribly wrong? Mom lost her apartment?"

"No, none of that."

"Then why don't you just tell me? If you want your friend to stay here, I get to know why."

This wasn't what I'd expected. She was acting like an uptight grown-up, not the crazy Upstairs Chloe I knew and loved. "You won't believe it," I said.

"Try me."

I turned to Sofie and Barrett. They gave me blank looks. Apparently this was up to me.

"Okay, but you have to promise not to tell anyone. Cross your heart and hope to die."

Chloe drew an X on her chest with her finger. "Hope to die if I breathe a word." She was grinning like mad. She thought I was hilarious.

"All right," I said. "I'll give you the short version. The long version is even more confusing."

"I'm sure it is. Go ahead. You have my full attention."

"Sofie is from Holland," I began. "But her parents died a long time ago and she's temporarily stuck here. Mom's in a really weird mood right now, as you no doubt noticed the other day, and I'm afraid if she knew about the situation, she'd call child services and they'd take Sofie away."

"*That's* your explanation?" Chloe said. "She's 'temporarily stuck here'?"

"It's the truth," I said. "Every word."

"Kind of like 'it's complicated'?"

"Yeah."

"No dice. Sorry, Joplin, but that's not enough."

I drooped like a wilting flower, right there on the Martinellis' lime-green couch. Chloe wasn't going to help. Worse, she'd probably run downstairs and tell Mom that I ought to see a therapist. That I was making up hare-brained stories about some homeless kid I'd picked up on the street because I was so desperate to have a friend.

Through all of this, Sofie hadn't moved a muscle,

except to drop her head a few inches. Barrett was giving me this *do something* look.

"C'mon, Chloe! Can't you just go with the flow?"

"*No*, Joplin, I can't *just go with the flow.* Are you insane?"

I actually thought about that for a nanosecond but decided I was not.

"Look—it's obvious that this is some kind of mess. And my dad would freak if I took in some runaway whose picture is up on the post office wall."

"Give me a break, Chloe! Does Sofie *look* like a runaway?"

She shrugged. "Who knows? They come in all flavors."

I stared down at my hands, my face burning. I'd screwed things up. Chloe wasn't budging and I couldn't shake the feeling that she was *absolutely* going to tell my mother. I tried to come up with something, but I kept hitting a wall.

And then it came to me.

"Chloe," I said, "I really *wish* you would help us."

She blinked a couple of times. "Sure," she said. "I'd be glad to."

Barrett spun around and glared at me. Sofie didn't move.

"Great!" I said. "Now, she'll be spending the weekend with me, so she'll move in with you on Sunday night. I'm going to tell Mom that she's your cousin from Cleveland and you're watching her while her parents are on vacation. I really *wish* you'd go along with that story. In case my mother asks."

"Of course," Chloe said. "No problem at all."

We walked down the stairs in absolute silence and out the entry door to the stoop. There Barrett sat down. I sat beside him. Sofie sat by me.

"I know what you're going to say," I said.

"Good. Because that was a terrible, really *dangerous* thing you just did."

"It worked, though. I wasn't sure it would."

"Is that how you make moral judgments? If it works? Because then it's okay to smash a store window and steal a camera—as long as you don't get caught. It worked. You got a free camera."

"*Excuse* me?"

"You totally don't get it, do you? Sofie *has* to grant your wishes. She has no choice, because something terrible happened to her. It's like she was enslaved in some magical way. And you took advantage of that."

"I did it to help *her.*"

"I know that. And I'm not saying you're a bad person."

"Oh, thanks!"

"But when you wished she was your friend and she suddenly appeared, you did that in complete innocence. But what you did just now, that was different. You *knew* you had the power and, without consulting Sofie or even really thinking it through, you used it. That's the really dangerous part. What's the chance you won't use it again? Get to like it."

He was right. I hadn't thought it through. Suddenly I felt sick.

I reached over and took Sofie's hand and squeezed it hard with both of mine. "I'm sorry," I said. "I'm so sorry! I won't do it again. Not ever."

She looked at me with those soulful, deep-water eyes but didn't say a thing. Not at first, anyway.

My natural instinct has always been to fill any silence in a conversation because they make me uncomfortable. But I had the feeling that Sofie needed to think things through before she spoke. So I forced myself to shut up and wait. Barrett did too.

Finally, when Sofie was ready, she said what was on her mind.

"Only one person has ever made me feel like a slave,"

she said softly. "And that was the person who enslaved me—I've never thought of it that way, Barrett, but it's a good analogy. Since then I've granted lots of wishes, but they were always innocent, like you wishing I was your friend, or well-intentioned, like what you did just now. But it *is* dangerous, Joplin. More than you know."

"I believe you, but I don't understand. Not really. It seems like your power to grant wishes could be used for good."

"I suppose. No one's ever wished for universal peace. But if they did, they'd be harnessing the forces of evil to do it."

I put my face in my hands and started to cry. Sofie put her arms around me. She was warm and soft, like the real flesh-and-blood person she was. I felt kindness and comfort in her hug. And then Barrett was reaching his long arms around both of us, and I knew that we were all right.

We would solve this problem.

13

The Mystery Man

Mom was in the kitchen, hunched over a pair of boneless, skinless chicken breasts on the cutting board. With the precision of a surgeon, she was slicing them into paper-thin cutlets.

"Mom?" I said softly. She finished that cutlet. Like the others, it was flawless.

"What?" she said, her attention still on the chicken, angling her knife for another pass. She'd been doing that a lot lately—talking *at* me, not bothering to look up.

"Can you put that down for a minute, please? I don't want to shock you into cutting off a finger."

She stood up straight and set down the knife. She had managed to smile and be cheerful while Barrett was around. Now that he'd gone home, she seemed unbearably tired. "What have you done now?"

"Nothing. I just made another friend. That's two in one day. Don't fall all over yourself with amazement."

"You need to stop doing that."

"Making friends?"

"No. Running yourself down. Acting so surprised when people like you."

"I'm just being realistic, Mom. Anyway, her name is Sofie. She's Upstairs Chloe's cousin from Cleveland and she's staying at the Martinellis' for a while. You'll like her."

"I'm sure I will."

"And I hope you don't mind—I know I should have asked you first—but I invited her to spend the weekend with us." Then, in a whisper, "Actually, she's already here."

"Here? Where?"

"In the living room."

"Oh, for heaven's sake, Joplin! Bring her in so I can meet her."

Mom washed the chicken goo off her hands while I went to get Sofie.

We'd carefully prepared for this moment, starting

with a makeover. I'd gone through my closet looking for the most generic items I owned, so Mom wouldn't notice they were mine. I'd chosen a denim skirt, a pale yellow tee, and ballet flats. Finally, we took out the braids and I gave her a ponytail. That transformed her completely. She looked like she belonged in the twenty-first century.

Next, we'd created a fictional life for Sofie, down to her street address in Cleveland, the school she attended, her full name—Sofie Ann Carlson—what her parents did for a living, and how they were related to Chloe. When we had it all figured out, I'd tested her by asking questions, pretending to be my mom. She hadn't made a single mistake.

So I was feeling really confident when I ushered Sofie into the kitchen.

Then suddenly things got weird.

Halfway in, she stopped in her tracks. Then she just stood there, gazing at Mom with what looked like amazement or surprise. Starting to panic, I turned to see how my mother was reacting and saw that Mom was staring at Sofie in exactly the same way, like she was searching her memory for something she couldn't quite grasp. And they went on like that, gazing and blinking like a couple of canaries studying their reflections in a mirror.

That moment felt like a lifetime, though it probably

lasted little more than two seconds, much longer than it took to tell. And then—*snap*! It was over.

"I'm sorry, Sofie," Mom said. "I didn't mean to be rude. You just looked so familiar, like someone I knew a long time ago. It took me by surprise."

Sofie nodded and smiled, but I could tell it took some effort. Then she took a deep breath and pulled herself together.

After that, things got normal again. Mom seemed instantly comfortable with Sofie. And Sofie not only remembered all the details of her fictional life in Cleveland, she seemed to have an instinct for what would interest my mom. Pretty soon they were chatting away like old friends. And for a precious few minutes our little apartment was filled with warmth and cheer. I couldn't have hoped for a better outcome.

Things were winding down and we were about to leave Mom to her chicken cutlets when we heard a key scrabbling in the lock.

"That'll be Jen," Mom said. "Excuse me." She went to the entry hall and knocked twice, our signal for "pull out the key; I'll unlock it from inside."

We heard the door open and shut.

"You're cutting it pretty close," Mom said, her voice floating over the sound of the bolt being set and the metallic clatter as the safety chain was fastened.

"I know," Jen said. "Traffic was a nightmare. And the vultures are still out there. Can you believe it? I mean, *what* can they possibly hope to—Oh, hi!" They'd come into the kitchen by then and she'd spotted Sofie. "I'm Jen."

"This is Joplin's new friend Sofie Carlson," Mom said. "She's Chloe's cousin and she'll be joining us for the weekend."

Jen's eyebrows shot up. "Wow, that's great! I really wish I didn't have to rush, but I have a gallery opening tonight and I have to go transform myself. But you'll be here all weekend, so we can talk later."

"Jen, wait," I called as she disappeared into the living room. "Will you and Leonard be coming back here after the party? Because we'll be taking some of the couch cushions into my room to make a bed for Sofie."

"Not to worry," she called back. "We're going out to dinner after. You girls enjoy your slumber party."

We hung around in the living room while Jen got dressed and Mom finished dinner. Sofie was eager to see how Jen would "transform" herself. Apparently this wasn't something she'd encountered over the course of her long, strange life.

"Don't get too excited," I said. "She doesn't turn into a princess or anything. Just, you know, fluffs her hair, puts on a black dress and high heels and dangly earrings."

"Does that make her look different?"

"Yeah, it kind of does. You'll see."

While we waited, Sofie's eyes wandered around the room. I wondered what she thought of Jen's collection of prints, which seemed a little strange, even to me. And things like the cordless phone and the flat-screen TV— did she even have a clue what they were? Did they have those things when she was a person before?

The house phone rang. I answered.

"Mom!" I called. "Can you talk to the agency guy?"

"Be right there," she called back.

I met her at the kitchen door and handed her the phone. She was drying her hands with a dishcloth, so she cradled the receiver between her ear and shoulder. "Hi, Eddie," she said.

I went back to the couch and whispered to Sofie, "Remember that man in the garden this morning? The one who was worried because you were hanging around near our door? He was one of our security guards. Mom's publisher hired them because these reporters have been stalking us. The agency phones in every night with a report."

"But why are reporters—?"

"All right," Mom said. "Hold on. I'll go look."

She disappeared into the kitchen, apparently going to look out the front window. "No, I've never seen him before," I heard her say on her way back into the living room. "Yes, I'm sure. Huh! That's odd."

I couldn't resist. I got up and headed for the door to take a look. Sofie was right behind me.

"I really don't know," Mom said. "Yeah. If you think that's best."

Careful not to show too much of my face, I peered out the window with one eye. Across the street, walking slowly and looking pointedly in our direction, was a short, stocky, middle-aged man. His brown hair was long over the ears. Bangs covered his forehead. As he shielded his eyes from the setting sun, the better to see our apartment, I caught the sparkle of gold and blue, and a little flash of red: the two rings on his right hand, one large and one small.

I sucked in breath, and for a moment I couldn't seem to let it out.

"Someone you know?" Sofie asked.

"Yes," I whispered. "His name is Lucius Doyle."

I remembered how eager he'd been to buy my "worthless" broken platter. How he'd offered me five hundred dollars and hinted that he might pay even more. How he'd flushed, and sweated, and trembled with emotion.

How he'd taken out his little book and written down my name and address.

"Can I see?"

"If you want." I slid away and let Sofie take my place. I was about to go tell Mom that I knew who the mystery man was, when Sofie reached over and grabbed my arm.

"*What?*"

"I know him too." Her voice was so soft I could barely hear.

"How could you?"

"His name wasn't Lucius Doyle then, but he's had many names over the years."

"Sofie, ow! You're hurting me."

"I'm sorry. But please don't go away."

"I won't."

She released my arm. "He's leaving now." She sounded terrified. She was trembling.

"Sofie, look at me. What you're saying doesn't make sense. There's no way you could possibly know that man. You've never been in New York before last night, and you haven't been anywhere except the garden and in this building. Maybe he just looks like—"

"No. It's him. And I *have* been here before. I was in New York a long time ago."

"When?"

"It doesn't matter. That's not the important thing."

Before I could ask what the important thing was, we heard the swish of a skirt and the click of high heels. And there was Jen in sapphire silk and sparkly fake-diamond earrings. She looked like a movie star.

It occurred to me for the first time that this wasn't one of her usual gallery openings, the ones she had to go to as part of her job. This was a special evening. She was like Cinderella going to the ball.

"You look amazing," I said.

"Excellent! That's exactly what I was aiming for. Will you lock up behind me?"

"Sure."

From the kitchen Mom called, "Have fun!"

Then Jen was gone, the door was secure, and we were alone in the hall.

"Okay," I said. "The important thing?"

Sofie seemed about to cry. She was hugging herself to stop the shivers.

"That man is the reason I'm here," she said. "He is the reason for everything."

It was like the clouds had parted and a bright ray of understanding shone right through. "Sofie—back when you knew him, was his name Hans van der Brock?"

She slid down the wall and sat on the floor. She

hunched over, head down, arms crossed over her chest. It was like her plane was going down and she was assuming the crash position.

"Was it?" I asked again.

"How did you know?" Her voice was very small.

"Come on," I said, reaching down with both hands to help her up. "We're going to my room now. Try to look normal."

14

Strawberry Fields

THE NEXT MORNING WE TOOK the subway up to Central Park—Sofie, Barrett, and me. Barrett had brought a rolled-up blanket and a picnic lunch for three.

He suggested we go to Strawberry Fields, since it was in a Beatles song and Barrett thought that was cool. There was a big mosaic set in the cement, with the word *Imagine* in the middle. Barrett said it was a memorial to John Lennon, who was arguably the most important Beatle.

I didn't know much about the Beatles, to be honest, and Sofie had never heard of them, but we stood and looked at the memorial for a while, sending good thoughts John Lennon's way, then wandered off toward the grass and trees.

There weren't any actual strawberries there, so far as I could tell, certainly not fields of them. But maybe there used to be, back in the day before it was a park. Or maybe they just called it that because of the song.

We found a nice, private spot under a shade tree and spread out the blanket. In the distance kids were playing Frisbee on the lawn. Couples were sitting under trees, kissing, or lying in the sun catching rays. People were out jogging, riding their bikes, reading, or walking their dogs. They all seemed happy to be in the park on a beautiful Saturday morning.

I didn't feel happy exactly, but I was strangely hopeful. Maybe it was the sunlight bouncing off the trees and the grass. Or maybe it was the way Sofie's hair was lit up from behind, like the halo on a Christmas card angel.

"Okay," I said to Barrett when we were settled. "There's a lot to tell."

Barrett nodded. He knew something big had gone down since he'd left on Friday afternoon. He just didn't know what.

"Sofie?" I said. "Why don't you start at the beginning, like you did last night?"

She sat up a little straighter. Her halo glowed even brighter.

"All right," she said. "You already know I come from Holland. I lived in a little village there, not far from the town of Delft. This was more than three hundred years ago. I had two older brothers, Hubert and Franz, and a little sister, Greta, who was still in her cradle, not yet a year old.

"We lived a simple life, or it would seem simple to you. My father was a carpenter, but like most country people we had a cow, some geese, a rooster, and some laying hens. My mother kept a kitchen garden. I helped with the housework and looked after Greta, who was the sweetest thing you could possibly imagine.

"It's Greta I miss the most. To think that she grew up, and lived her whole life, and died, and I never saw any of it—that's very sad for me."

I reached over and squeezed her hand. Sofie squeezed back.

"There was a market every week in the next village over. It wasn't far, an hour's walk, I would guess. Sometimes my mother would send me there with things to sell—eggs, mostly, cheese, and little cakes she made. I would buy things we needed with the money I got.

"I passed many cottages along the way. But on the

outskirts of this other village there was one house that was noticeably larger than the others. It belonged to a potter—he needed more space for his workshop, you see, and his kiln. His name was Hans van der Brock, and he used to stand outside his door smoking his long pipe and watching the people pass by. I didn't know this till later, but he was looking for interesting faces, getting ideas for the pictures he painted on the china he made. It's something artists do.

"One day he asked if I would pose for him. All I had to do was stand still while he drew my picture. He said he'd give me a penning—it wasn't much, like your penny, but it seemed quite generous to me, especially for doing nothing. So I did what he asked and he paid me as promised. After that it became a regular thing, almost every week."

"He was trying to gain your trust," Barrett guessed.

"That's right. Then one day he offered to pay me a stuiver, a much larger amount, if I would pose a bit longer. As you said, I had come to trust him by then. He'd even told me to call him Hans, like we were old friends. Anyway, I agreed.

"In the past, we'd always just stood in the yard while he sketched, and it was pretty quick. But this time he brought me into his workshop. He showed me exactly how to stand. I was to pretend I'd just led my geese to a pond, then someone had called my name, so I turned toward the sound. 'Just so,' he said, turning my shoulders at an angle. 'Give me a half smile, like you're glad to see your friend.'

"This time he didn't draw with charcoal. He painted directly on the platter with a tiny brush. The whole time he kept muttering to himself, saying words in a strange language I had never heard before. When he'd finished painting, he sprinkled some powders over the platter—three different kinds. The first was yellow and smelled like rotten eggs. The next one was white. And the last was blue—just a pinch, as they say in recipes."

Sofie pressed her thumb and pointer together to demonstrate.

"The next thing I knew, I wasn't standing anymore. I was looking straight up into his face—from below and very close. I couldn't move. I couldn't breathe. It was like I didn't have a body at all. I had become part of the platter.

"I stared up at his face as he finished the platter, painting in the background and all the other details. He had a square sort of head and a big, fleshy nose. His eyes frightened me the most. They were this startling blue, so pale they were almost transparent, like water in a clear stream.

"Finally, when he'd finished, he carried the platter outside and put it into the fiery kiln."

"Oh!" Barrett said, flinching and sucking in breath. I scooted in closer and, without letting go of Sofie's hand, grabbed Barrett's too.

"I was terrified—well, you can imagine. But I felt no pain at all. I just knew where I was and what was happening around me. Inside the kiln it was all fire and dancing light, as I'd always imagined the mouth of hell would be."

I looked over at Barrett, who shuddered. I remembered how hard it had been for me to hear that story the first time—in whispers, in the darkness of my room at night.

"Finally, after the oven had cooled, he took the platter out again. He seemed very pleased with his creation. 'Now listen, Sofie,' he said, looking directly at me. 'I wish to be a wealthy man. I want you to do that for me.'

"And so it began. He had many wishes after that, and I fulfilled them all. Or rather, as I told you yesterday, the things he wanted flowed through me and out to him."

"But I don't understand why he needed you at all." Barrett was leaning forward now, gazing at her intently. "Why couldn't he just do his magic all by himself and grant his own wishes?"

"I've asked myself that same question many times. I can only guess that for the magic to work, he needed to capture a spirit."

"Sort of like Faust?" Barrett asked.

Sofie cocked her head. "What is that?"

"An old story, about a man who made a pact with the devil—his soul in exchange for riches, and love, and all the knowledge in the world."

"But this isn't the same," I said. "Even assuming the Faust story was scientific and not a fairy tale. Sofie didn't sell anything or get anything. She was kidnapped and enslaved."

"Right," Barrett said. "But I'd still like to think that when Van der Brock died, he was dragged kicking and screaming into a fiery pit."

"I would like to think that too," Sofie said. "It would be justice. But I'm afraid he is in no danger of dying anytime soon."

"What?"

"I'll get to that in a minute, Barrett. But it's best if I tell things as they happened."

Sofie had her own particular way of speaking. Always kind of formal and solemn. And she laid out her thoughts in an orderly manner. They flowed like a story.

I guess all those years of watching and listening had made her that way. Not to mention the long, boring hours she'd spent staring at walls in empty rooms. She must have gone deep into her mind then, thinking about the people she'd seen, the things they said and did. Making stories from their lives, and her own.

"I'm not sure what happened in the weeks that followed," Sofie went on. "Hans put the platter away in a drawer, wrapped in layers of cloth. I could hear things, but just barely, and I saw nothing at all.

"The people of my village would have searched for me. They might even have gone to Van der Brock's workshop, since the neighbors knew I posed for him. We stood outside while he sketched, where everyone could see. But they wouldn't have looked for me inside a drawer.

"I thought about that constantly, there in the darkness—how my parents must have suffered. If I had died of disease, as so many children did, of course they would have been sad. But it would have seemed natural. To simply disappear—that was alarming."

Barrett reached over and took her free hand. We formed a circle now, holding hands.

"Some time later, we moved from the village to a house in some great city. I think it was probably Amsterdam, though I never knew for sure. It was far from Delft, though. I heard Hans mention that several times, that he was glad to get away from that place.

"Once we were in the city, he took the platter out of its wrapping and put it on display. He'd kept it hidden in the village, of course, because the people there might recognize my face. But in Amsterdam, or wherever we were, he felt perfectly safe. So after that I could see and hear what went on around me.

"Hans was a rich man by then. His house was very grand, filled with expensive furnishings—Turkish carpets, fine paintings, silver goblets and candle stands, tapestries hanging on the walls. He dressed in silk and velvet, with gold buttons on his jackets, plumes in his hats.

"He had set the platter on a cupboard in the room where he dined with his guests, so I heard their conversations. That's how I know about his circle of friends. They were alchemists, men who dabbled in sorcery and read forbidden books. Even I, a country girl with no education, knew how dangerous that was. They burned people for such crimes back then—burned or drowned.

"One morning a man came to the house. I'd seen him many times before. But that day, he was frightened and in a hurry. He was leaving the city, he said, and Hans was advised to do the same, because one of their mutual friends had been arrested for witchcraft. People knew of their connections, that the accused man had often visited the Van der Brock house. Both of them were likely to be arrested next. It would be wise to get away before that happened.

"As soon as the man had gone, Hans burned all his

suspicious books and the pages and pages of notes he'd carefully written. Then he took passage under a false name on a ship bound for New York. It was called New Amsterdam back then. Lots of Dutch people lived there.

"But, of course, they burned witches in the New World too. So, to be absolutely safe, Hans made a wish for immortality. No matter what they might do to him, he would not die."

"You're telling me he's *still alive?*"

Sofie nodded.

"We saw him yesterday," I said, "right outside our apartment."

For once, Barrett was speechless.

"And there's more. *I* recognized him too. He calls himself Lucius Doyle now. He has a fancy antiques shop over on Bedford. And *that's* where Jen took me to have the platter mended! But there was something about him that creeped me out, so we left—but not before he'd written down my name and address."

This was too much for Barrett to absorb. He got up and walked in circles again, as he had the day before.

One of the things I'd liked about Barrett right from the start was how he cared so deeply about things. He *loved* books, he was *excited* about science, and he was a *huge* fan of Sherlock Holmes. So it made sense that he'd care just as deeply about his friends and their problems—which made me like him even more than I already did.

After a while he came back and sat down. "Okay," he said. "Keep going."

"Well, Hans had learned his lesson about showing off his wealth. So he set himself up as an ordinary tradesman. He opened a shop that sold Dutch china and settled in to live a quiet life. He lived comfortably, you understand, but he wasn't ostentatious.

"After about twenty years, he packed up and moved to a different neighborhood, changed his name, and started over again with a new shop, new friends, a whole new life. This happened over and over. You see, he was afraid that people would notice that he never got any older. And once they started wondering why, he would be in danger again.

"Being immortal had consequences he hadn't considered before. It wasn't just that he had to keep moving and reinventing himself. He met women he fancied, for example, but he could never marry or have a normal family life. Imagine—his children and grandchildren would grow old and die and he would not have changed at all. He was stuck, same as me. I believe he came to regret his wish."

"Couldn't he just unwish it, then?" Barrett asked.

"I expect he could have. But before he had absolutely made up his mind, he lost possession of the platter."

"Was it stolen?"

"No, and that's a very important point. Because only the legitimate owner of the platter can harness its power. If it had been stolen, Hans could still have gone on making wishes, no matter where it might be. But this was a legitimate sale. The platter was sold by the shop assistant and paid for in cash. It was just a foolish mistake.

"You see, Hans—or Thomas Quince, as he was called then—had gone out for lunch, and his assistant sold it to one of their regular customers, a wealthy merchant. I guess there had been so many shops by then, and so many assistants, that Hans had somehow forgotten to tell *this particular* man that the platter hanging on the wall behind his desk was never to be sold.

"He was very angry when he found out. He went to the merchant's house to buy it back. But the man refused to part with it, probably because Hans made a fuss and lost his temper. Things got so heated that the merchant's wife sent a servant down to the street to summon the police.

"That was the last time I saw Hans until last night. The merchant sent the platter to Providence as a gift to his son. Over the years it passed from hand to hand, place to place. I believe Hans has been searching for it ever since. Now he's found it and—"

"Sofie?" Barrett said. "Excuse me for interrupting, but there's a man sitting over there—*don't turn around!*—who's been reading the same page of the newspaper for, like, twenty minutes."

"What does he look like?"

"Hard to tell. He's mostly hidden behind the paper. Also, he's wearing a baseball cap and it casts a shadow over his face. But there's definitely something strange about him."

"Like what?"

"His jeans are baggy and too long, like they don't really fit him. And they still have the creases from the store. Also his sneakers are new. I think he bought those clothes so he'd blend in at the park."

"Barrett," I said, "can you see his hands?"

"Yeah."

"On the right hand, does he have a big ring on his index finger, gold with a blue stone?"

"Yes."

"Another one on his little finger?"

"I see something gold. It's hard to see from here."

"We need to get out of here right now."

15

Whatever It Takes

Our uneaten lunches were still in the Gristedes bag. So we moved the bag aside and shook out the blanket, and Barrett calmly rolled it back up. Then we strolled away from Strawberry Fields toward the Seventy-Second Street station—cool and calm, like we didn't have a worry in the world.

Like we weren't being stalked by a four-hundred-year-old demonic magician.

As soon as we were out of sight, we broke into a run.

I gripped Sofie's hand as we raced down the stairs to the subway station, out of the sunlight, and into the eerie, fluorescent-lit darkness. It occurred to me about halfway down that the whole escape thing was pointless. Lucius Doyle didn't need to follow us. He already knew where I lived.

Even so, I was glad he still hadn't appeared on the platform when the train came into the station. And I didn't mind when Barrett got all Sherlock Holmes and had us get off at Columbus Circle, switch to the D train, get off at Rockefeller Center, wait for the next train, then get back on. It was all pretty silly, like something out of a movie, but also kind of exciting. And when we came back up at the West Fourth Street station, Lucius Doyle was nowhere to be seen.

We walked over to Washington Square Park to eat our lunches. Barrett suggested we sit near the tables where the local chess freaks played speed games for money. Lots of people hung around to watch them play, so there would be safety in numbers. If Doyle should suddenly appear, he wouldn't bother us in public.

I'd watched the speed games in the park before, and I still couldn't imagine anyone figuring out a chess move that fast. Their hands were absolutely flying, plopping their pieces down and hitting the timer in no more than a second. You'd have to be a genius to do that. Or have a mind like a computer, with every chess move prepro-grammed and ready to use.

I wondered what it would be like to have a mind like that. Would everybody you meet seem unbearably stupid and slow? And were they all-around geniuses, or just brilliant about chess?

"Earth to Joplin," Barrett said.

"Sorry. Did you say something?"

"I was just wondering why Doyle would go to all that trouble—disguising himself, following us to the park, hiding behind a newspaper. What did he have to gain?"

"The thing he wants most in the world," I said. "The platter and the power to make wishes again."

Barrett shook his head. "He already knows where the platter is. And he can't steal it—or rather he could, but it wouldn't do him any good. He could try to force you into giving it back, but he didn't do that either. He just sat there and watched us talk. He couldn't hear what we said. He was too far away. So what was the point?"

"He learned a lot, actually," Sofie said. "First of all, he saw me with you. So he knows that Joplin has discovered the power of his magic and has wished for me to become a person again. That in itself is an important discovery. And watching our conversation in the park—mostly me talking, the two of you listening, and seeing how you reacted to what I said—that was useful too. Even though he couldn't hear our words, it will be obvious to him that I was telling you my story. So now it's clear what he's up against, and that there isn't an easy solution. Tricking Joplin into selling him the platter is no longer an option.

"What he *doesn't* know is that we saw him outside the apartment last night—*both of us* did—so we figured out that Lucius Doyle and Hans are one and the same. And that we recognized him at the park just now. He'll build his strategy based on the information he has—and we have more than he does."

"What sort of strategy?"

"I don't know. Whatever it takes to get what he wants."

When we got to the apartment, the cushions were back on the couch, Jen was awake and sitting next to Leonard, and Mom was pouring champagne into tall, skinny glasses. There was a huge arrangement of flowers on the coffee table and bowls of nuts and olives and chips. It was like they were having a very small party.

"Um, we're back?" I said from the doorway, a little confused.

Jen waved us in. "Come celebrate," she said.

"Okay. What are we celebrating?"

"Wedded bliss: Leonard and I are getting married!"

"Oh," I said.

That was, of course, the wrong thing to say, and the wrong way to say it. I could see surprise mixed with disappointment written all over Jen's face. Leonard actually blushed. And Mom gave me a stern look of warning.

I knew it was mean and selfish of me to act like that on Jen's special day, but the news had hit me really hard. My feelings were already churned up about Mom; I was worried about Sofie and scared of Lucius Doyle. Now, on top of all that, I got to be heartsick too. Because Jen getting married meant Jen would move away. And I couldn't imagine just me and my mother living there alone, especially since she'd gotten all weird and depressed. Jen was the glue that held us together, the peanut butter in our sandwich. Without her, we'd fall apart.

"That's great!" I finally managed to say. But it came much too late and sounded horribly fake.

"Joplin," Jen said, "the wedding isn't till next spring. And we're just moving to the Upper West Side, not Australia."

I nodded stupidly and tried to smile as I sat there feeling heavy and cold, every ounce of joy draining out of me. Apparently I was draining all the joy out of the party too, because Mom rushed in to fill the silence and smooth things over. She introduced my friends to Leonard, topped off his champagne, and searched her mind for some way to pull me out of my mood.

"Abby dropped by this morning," she said, hitting me with her laser gaze. "I told her you'd gone to the park *with your friends*."

This time my smile was real. "What'd she want?"

"To see you. She said she'd come back tomorrow. She looked . . . what's the word?"

"Wretched?" Jen suggested.

"Pitiful? Desolate? Hangdog?" Leonard tried, clearly relieved by the change of subject.

"*Wretched* will do. So be kind to her when she comes— okay?"

"Yeah," I said. "Sure. Can't wait."

More awkward silence followed. Leonard ran his fingers through the tight, black curls of his very short hair. Then he picked up a bowl of cashews and offered them around—first to Jen and Mom, then to Sofie, Barrett, and me.

I'm not proud of this, just so you know. But I couldn't bear that he was acting like the host. He didn't live with us. He wasn't part of our family. So I pretended like I didn't notice him standing there holding out the bowl.

Finally he put it down, sighed softly, and went back to sit next to Jen.

I don't know what Barrett and Sofie thought of my behavior—that I was being a little brat, probably. Or maybe they knew me better than I knew myself. Saw that I was sick with grief and desperately needed some help. Needed, at the very least, to think of something besides *once again* losing my best friend.

So Barrett leaned over and whispered in my ear, reminding me of what we'd discussed on our way back to the apartment. We'd all agreed that, as long as we went about it carefully, there was no harm in telling Mom the identity of the mystery man. And it might buy us some added protection.

I nodded and did my best to pull myself together.

"Oh, Mom," I said. "Remember that call last night from the security people?"

"Yes."

"The man he asked you about, the one who's been lurking around outside? Well, I know who he is."

"Seriously?"

"Yes. Sofie and I went and looked out the window, remember? It was Lucius Doyle, the guy who was going to repair my platter."

"No!" Jen was shocked. *"Really?"*

"Absolutely positive. I saw him, clear as day."

"Apparently he's been passing by a lot," Mom said, "multiple times a day, always slowing down when he gets close to our apartment. When there are reporters around, he tries to blend in with them. And he always invents some excuse to stop—lights up a cigarette and stands there to smoke it, or makes a really long call on his cell. But what he's actually doing is watching us."

"Well, you don't know the half of it," I said, and launched into the story of our visit to Lucius Doyle—his increasingly extravagant offers to buy my "worthless" broken platter, the sweating and panting, and the fact that he reminded me of the devil.

"Sounds like he's planning a robbery," Leonard said.

Jen agreed. "Sounds that way to me too. Remember what we talked about after we left?" she said to me. "How he had that look like he'd just hit the jackpot? That platter must be pretty rare, worth a lot of money, for a man like him to even consider stealing it."

"*And*," I said, holding up my hand to say that I wasn't finished yet, "guess who showed up in Central Park this morning."

"You're kidding me!" Jen was absolutely crushed. After all, she had taken me to his shop, setting this whole thing in motion.

"Lucius Doyle. In disguise. Spying on us."

"He was hiding behind a newspaper," Barrett said, holding up an imaginary *New York Times*. "He had on this 'ordinary guy' getup—new jeans, new sneakers, a Yankees cap. Maybe he knew your security people had spotted him, so he was trying to be inconspicuous."

Mom shot to her feet. "I'm calling the agency right now," she said, grabbing the phone and punching in the numbers.

I had no problem with that. None at all. Because the thought of Doyle working on some unnamed "strategy"—*whatever it takes to get what he wants*—made chills run along my arms and up to the top of my head.

By the time Mom hung up, Eddie had promised to investigate Lucius Doyle. A third agent would be brought in to tail him the next time he passed by.

I wondered what they'd find.

Back in the olden days, when Hans started changing his identity every twenty years or so, it probably wasn't that hard. All he had to do was pick a new name and move across town to a different neighborhood. Maybe tell his friends, assuming he had any, that he was moving to Boston or someplace like that, so they wouldn't wonder why he'd suddenly disappeared.

But it wouldn't be that easy in the modern world.

There was public information on file about everyone—birth certificates, social security numbers, school records, email accounts, credit card histories, tax records, phone accounts, rental contracts—and computers to search for it. You'd have to be as smart as those chess freaks in the park to reinvent yourself that many times and not leave a trail.

And Doyle hadn't even had the option of moving somewhere far away—to another state, another country. He'd needed to stay in New York and keep working in the antiques trade, so he'd know if any old Dutch platters just happened to come up for sale. It was his only chance to undo that fateful wish.

"I'll walk you to school for a while," Mom said. "Till we get this thing sorted out. Just to make sure you're safe."

"No, please!" I said, horrified. "Don't!"

"What—are you afraid the kids will tease you?"

"*Yes!*"

"And that's more important than your safety?"

"You just hired an agent to follow him. I'll be plenty safe."

"I'm not sure I'm comfortable with that."

From across the room Jen made a little chopping motion with her hands, and Mom got the message. "Just be careful, then—all right?"

"I will, Mom. Don't worry." I shot Jen a quick smile of gratitude and resolved to be kind to Leonard from that moment on. Fair was fair.

Soon they went back to talking about the wedding, and for a while, we just sat there chowing down on the cashews. Leonard had left the bowl right in front of us, and we just kept reaching for more until they were gone.

"We're going to my room," I said. And, judging by the grown-ups' startled expressions, apparently I cut Leonard off in midsentence. Only this time I hadn't done it on purpose. I just wasn't paying attention to their conversation.

"I'm sorry, Leonard," I said. "I didn't mean to interrupt. Really, really, really!"

He looked up and smiled. Gave me a little nod.

I'd talk to Jen about it later, explain why I'd been such a bear. She'd understand. She always did.

Sofie and Barrett got up, muttering polite things. When we left, the room was dead silent and it lasted for a long time. I know because I stood with my ear pressed against my closed bedroom door, hearing nothing, picturing them mouthing words and making faces.

Then, finally, Leonard's voice.

"Whoa, what happened to all those cashews?"

16

Still Warm
from the Oven

Sunday lunch was a tradition in Barrett's family. His dad always cooked a roast and the grandparents came, along with an aunt and uncle and a bunch of cousins. That day Barrett left as soon as he could without hurting anybody's feelings, but it was almost two before he got to our apartment.

"Sorry," he said. "It sort of went on and on. But I brought you this." It was a brown paper grocery bag, rolled at the top. He opened a corner of the bag and held it out to me. "Close your eyes and take a whiff."

So I did. I smelled apples, cinnamon, and pastry, with

maybe a hint of lemon peel. I did an over-the-moon eye roll and gave him a dreamy sigh.

Then it was Sofie's turn. She leaned down and sniffed, as I had, but her response was altogether different. She seemed shocked, or amazed, or full of wonder. I couldn't quite tell which.

"What?" I said.

"It smells like home."

"You mean *home* home?"

"Yes. Oh! It makes me shiver all over."

"We'll get you back there, don't worry," I said, reaching out and giving her a squeeze.

And I meant it too—totally and sincerely. But it would have been more honest to say we'd give it our best try. That's all I could really promise.

"There's enough for everybody," Barrett said, pulling out an aluminum dish containing most of an apple pie and setting it proudly on the kitchen table. "Mom made two of these—*two!*—then half the family announced that they were on diets. All kinds, you name it. My cousin Adele claims she's allergic to sugar. They just sat there while the rest of us ate dessert. Dad had two slices just to make my mom feel better."

I got out plates, forks, and a knife. Barrett cut the pieces. Then we stood there in the kitchen eating pie.

It was much better than the kind you get from a bakery. The crust was crisp and salty-sweet, still warm from the oven. It was everything good about homemade—not perfect, better than perfect. The rim had the imprint of his poet mother's fingers, where she'd squeezed the pastry into sharp little waves. And the lattice shone with crystals of sugar that sparkled like tiny jewels.

"Your mother is a genius," I said.

"I'll tell her you said that. It'll make up for the relatives and their stupid diets."

We saved a piece for Jen, who was out with Leonard, and took one to Mom, who was working in her room.

For some reason, it overwhelmed her. Maybe it was the way Barrett brought it in, like a waiter in a fancy restaurant—bowing, one hand behind his back. She gave a little laugh, but it was the kind that had tears behind it. The whole thing was so unexpected and so sweet, a beautiful little slice of home, or love, or happiness.

She just held it in her hands and looked up at us, sitting there in front of my grandfather's typewriter, confused.

"Enjoy!" Barrett said, backing out of the room. We closed the door very gently and went out to the garden.

"I think you just made her day," I said.

"I dunno. She looked kind of sad."

"That's how she always looks these days. Or most of the time, anyway."

"I'm sorry," he said.

"Yeah. Me too."

"Do you know why she's sad?"

"No, except that she's wallowing in her past. She can't seem to get out of it, and won't talk about it either. Not even to Jen, and for sure not to me."

Sofie pulled me close, leaned her head on my shoulder, her hair tickling my cheek. It was exactly what I needed just then—my bosom friend.

I had two of them, in fact. What were the chances?

We sat in the usual place, though I noticed that the grass was starting to get matted and made a mental note to pick a different spot next time. It was my garden, and it was beautiful. I wanted to keep it that way.

We talked about the pie and how people were getting so picky about food—anything except the problem we couldn't seem to solve.

Sofie was even quieter than usual. She mostly just looked down at her lap and fiddled with a blade of grass. I think she was silently saying good-bye to her hopes.

"You know," Barrett said, pointing in the air with his

index finger, as if the solution was floating right above us, "I've been thinking."

Sofie and I looked up at him, as hopeful as a pair of puppies whose human had just produced a treat. If we'd had tails, we would have wagged them.

"About what?" I said.

"Lucius Doyle. It was scary that he followed us. And creepy that he actually went to the trouble of disguising himself. But I've gone round and round, trying to figure out what his strategy might be, and I don't see any way he can harm us."

"Why not?"

"Well, he won't try to steal the platter, we know that. There'd be no point."

We nodded agreement.

Now he turned to me. "And let's say he tried to hurt Sofie—or me, or your mom, or Jen—as a way of forcing you to sell him the platter. All you'd have to do is wish us away to safety. And if he went after you for the same reason, you could wish yourself to safety. You could even wish something bad would happen to him. Whatever you did, he wouldn't die, but it would hurt and it would set him back for a while. Don't you see? *You have all the power.*"

"Sadly, no," I said. "Because he's the only one who can set Sofie free."

"Are you absolutely sure of that? Beyond any doubt?" We both looked at Sofie.

"As sure as I can be about anything," she said.

Barrett sighed. "It's ironic. Kind of like *The Gift of the Magi*—you have what he needs and he has what you need, and it's not doing either of you any good."

"And there's something else in his favor," I said, getting more depressed by the minute. "He has all the time in the world to get his hands on the platter. Literally. He just has to wait long enough."

"Yes," Sofie said. "That's true. And if somehow, years and years from now, he *does* get the platter and make his wish—"

She couldn't finish. The thought was too horrible to speak. Because if Lucius Doyle became mortal again, finished out the span of his life, and died—Sofie would be trapped forever in her moment of time. There'd be no one left with the power to set her free.

I had not even considered this till that moment. But once I had, it washed over me like a tsunami, leaving me breathless. This really was Sofie's last chance. We *had* to figure something out. It was a hanging-by-your-fingernails-from-a-cliff-edge crisis, a baby-in-the-street-with-a-truck-coming emergency.

And it was just at this terrifying moment—that is to

say, the worst possible time for an interruption—that the back door opened and Mom peered out. Before she could say, "Abby's here," my former best friend was through the door and headed our way.

No, I thought. *No, no, no, not now!*

But here she came, homing in on us like a guided missile. She saw the three of us sitting in a circle on the grass—me and my new friends—and for a moment she hesitated.

Good, I thought. *Some other time, please. Just go away now.*

But she bucked up and kept on coming.

I got this acid feeling in my stomach. I didn't want another apology from Abby. I didn't even want to think about her just then. All the same, I had to admire her persistence. It couldn't be easy for her, standing outside the little boxwood border, gazing down at us. And the look on her face was so pitiful that I scooted over and made a space for her on the grass. When she didn't move, I patted it and gave her a nod. She stepped into our private circle and sat down.

"Abby, these are my friends, Barrett Browning and Sofie Carlson."

"I remember you," Barrett said. "From the library." It was obvious from the way he said it that he didn't remember her fondly.

"Yes. I was there," Abby said, stiff as a stump. "And that was a mean thing to do. Everything we did was mean. But I was worse than the others because Joplin was my friend."

"Not anymore, though," Barrett said. "So I guess that makes it okay."

I gasped. I didn't know Barrett had it in him to be cruel.

"No, it isn't okay," Abby said. "Joplin, I know I already told you I was sorry. But that was something we *had* to do. This is my real apology."

"The posh girls kick you out?"

"Let it go, Barrett," I said. He wasn't helping. He made me cringe.

"No, that's a fair question. They didn't exactly 'kick me out.' They just, you know, ignore me now."

I thought about that for a moment. I'd been wrong about Angelina. She hadn't gotten Abby to turn on me to test her loyalty to the group. Abby was never even considered. They were just playing with her like a cat that's got hold of a mouse. For their amusement.

"Abby—I'm really sorry things didn't work out, with me or the Fashionistas. But it was nice of you to come here and say what you did. I know it must have been hard."

"I still want to be your friend." It came out of her mouth and landed with a thud. I'd been feeling sorry for her and was willing to be nice. Now I was angry again.

"Even though we have 'nothing in common'?"

"Oh, Joplin, that was my mom. She was on me all summer about 'making some changes,' getting in with the 'right girls,' learning how to act and how to dress. She made it sound like my whole future depended on it."

"She's been saying that stuff for years. You used to think it was funny."

"Well, she amped it up really loud since then. She just wouldn't stop. Then I got back to school and Angelina was suddenly all interested in me. It just kind of happened."

I stared at her, appalled.

"No, Abby, it wasn't your mom who said those things to me. It was you. And if you can't think for yourself, if you let your mom tell you what to say and do—well, I'm sorry, but that's really sad. You'll grow up to be exactly like her. Who knows, maybe you can have your own gilded ceiling someday."

She was horrified. So was I, but I couldn't stop myself.

"And just for the record, it didn't 'just kind of happen.' *You* made that choice. So if you're coming here pretending that this is an apology, and then you rewrite history so it sounds like you were actually innocent, well . . . it would *really* help if you took some responsibility for what you did."

Now she was crying, like she had on the phone, and it made me sick. But she still wouldn't leave. I swear, I could have whacked her over the head with one of Jen's golf clubs and she would have just sat there and taken it.

"I'm not as good a person as you," she said when she'd finally stopped sobbing. "Not as smart, either. That's why I always followed your lead. It wasn't just that you had all the fun ideas. You always knew what was right."

Deep in my heart I understood two things: (1) Abby was trying to win a point by shamelessly flattering me, and (2) she was more or less right. I *was* smarter and more creative than Abby. Maybe that's why it had worked so well for as long as it did. She needed a leader and I wanted to be the boss (which, now that I thought about it, didn't make me sound so great either). And though I didn't *always* know what was right, at least I bothered to ask the question.

"Well," I said, desperately wanting the whole hideous moment to be over, "it was nice of you to say that. And brave of you to come here. Now it's done. You don't ever have to apologize again."

She still sat there.

"And the thing is, we have some really important

business right now. Maybe we could talk later?"

"All right," she said, getting to her feet. Her face was mottled red and she looked like she might throw up. But boy, was she hanging in there! I wouldn't have thought she had it in her. "See you at school?"

"Sure," I said.

She waved good-bye, then made her way across the garden without once looking back. We watched her in silence, the way people stare at an accident.

"That was amazing," Sofie said. "She was very brave."

"Yes," I agreed.

And what had I been?

"Hold on a minute," I said, getting up. "Be right back."

Mom was just unlatching the door to let Abby out when I came scampering into the entry hall.

"Wait!" I said. "I have something for you."

Abby blinked and Mom shot me a curious look. I ran to the kitchen, scooped Jen's slice of pie off the plate, and wrapped it carefully in foil. But I didn't seal it completely shut. I left a corner open.

"Shut your eyes and take a whiff," I said.

Abby looked at me, not the foil-wrapped package. Silently, she was asking: *Is this a joke? Is it going to be dog turds or something?*

"Go ahead," I said.

So she did. She sniffed, and almost fainted with relief.

Not a joke.

It was a gift.

Tears were trickling down her cheeks again. But this time I was pretty sure they were tears of happiness.

"Eat it on the way home," I suggested. "It's still warm from the oven."

"I will," she squeaked, then ducked out the door.

17

A Really Ugly Lady

School on Monday started out bad and went downhill from there. It had nothing to do with bullies. I was *so* over that old drama by then, I could have eaten Fashionistas for breakfast. My mind was on bigger things: the problem of evil, the perils of immortality, and this really bad feeling I had.

At first I was just fretting about Sofie, alone all day in a stranger's apartment with nothing to do except wait for me. Granted, she'd spent several hundred years just staring at walls and waiting for things to happen, so she ought to be used to it by now. And it was better now that she was a real person. She could take a nice hot bath, or make a sandwich, or get lost in a really good book—though she was probably too polite to go through the Martinellis' bookshelves looking for something to read.

That's how my mind was running: round and round in circles like a dog chasing its tail. On one hand, things were terrible. On the other, they could have been worse. Round and round and round I went. But as the morning progressed the circles got bigger and brought in more worries.

That's when the *really bad feeling* started, first as a prickling at the back of my neck, then these tight little twitches of anxiety. I couldn't exactly define my fear, but it really troubled me. As every minute passed I grew increasingly desperate to get home and make sure Sofie was all right.

I kept telling myself there was no reason she shouldn't be. I'd taken her to Chloe's after dark the night before, and we'd made sure that Lucius Doyle wasn't lurking around before we went outside. There was no way he could possibly know where Sofie was. He'd assume she was still in our apartment.

Then, in the middle of language arts, my fear finally announced itself: Barrett and I had completely missed the great big hole in his logic. Yes, I could wish Sofie to safety if Lucius Doyle tried to harm her—*but only if I knew it had happened*. What if he'd snatched her that morning, right after Chloe left? I wouldn't find out until hours later, when I got home from school.

When the bell rang for third period, I dashed to the front office and asked to use the phone. I didn't have a cell phone, and even if I had, we weren't supposed to bring them to school. The office lady was our lifeline.

When I said I needed to "call a sick friend," she gave me this knowing look, like that was probably the lamest excuse she'd ever heard—and no doubt she'd heard them all. But however grouchy she may have appeared, she was basically a pushover, and everybody knew it. She let me make the call.

Sofie didn't answer. I just got Dr. and Dr. Martinelli's voice mail. So I hung up and called again, thinking she'd figure it was important and might pick up this time. Still no luck.

"I guess she's asleep," I said to the office lady, then slumped down the hall to my next class. By then my anxiety had risen a couple more notches.

True, Sofie really could have been asleep. Or in the bathroom. Or, more likely, she didn't think she should answer someone else's phone. Or maybe she didn't know how to answer—all those mystifying buttons.

At lunch, Barrett said I was overreacting. He explained once again why Sofie was safe. And though he agreed there'd been a hole in his logic, he didn't think it mattered, because Lucius Doyle had nothing to gain by bothering Sofie—even if he knew where she was, which he didn't.

Still, I couldn't stop fretting. Disaster scenarios kept popping into my head. The day dragged on, unbearable.

When the last bell rang I was out the door like a shot. I didn't even go by my locker to change out my books. Hang homework. I needed to get home.

To my astonishment, as I was speed walking down Christopher Street, there came Abby trotting after me. A few seconds later, she'd caught up. She must have skipped the locker visit too.

"I hope you don't mind," she said, a little out of breath. "I can walk home another way if you'd rather."

"No," I lied. "It's fine."

She'd been smiling shyly at me all day, but otherwise had kept to herself. At lunch she'd gone off to eat in her lonely, post-Fashionista limbo—probably at Oscar's table, where they let anybody in. It was mostly boys, though, and they mostly talked about video games and what levels they were on.

I knew this because I'd sat there myself before

discovering the wonders of lunch in the library. Now I had a place to eat and Barrett Browning too. Compared to Abby, I was lucky. And watching her desperately jogging along, trying to keep up with me on those short little legs, I felt sorry for her—really, genuinely sorry.

We followed our same old route, the one Mom had taught me in third grade: Hudson up to Charles, then Charles over to West Fourth. That was the corner where we'd meet in the mornings and part in the afternoons. It reminded me of the good times, when Abby was still my bosom friend.

We had this game we'd play while we walked, called "If I had a billion dollars." Basically, it was a competition to see who could spend their money in the most outrageous way. My all-time best effort was a room built entirely of fish tanks, with a glass ceiling, so you could see the sky. Abby's was an electric train that would run through her ginormous house, since it'd take hours to walk from the multiple living rooms to the bedroom suite.

Now, as she walked beside me, I couldn't find my way back to that sort of easy conversation. The connections had all been broken. And the longer we walked in silence, the more awkward it got.

Finally, Abby said, "That pie was amazing."

"Yeah, it was. Barrett's mother made it." The minute

I said it, it sounded wrong, like a reminder that I had friends, when she did not.

"He's really cute."

"Yeah, I think so too."

"Is he your boyfriend?"

I sighed, my sympathy fading, annoyance taking its place.

"I'm *eleven*," I snapped. "I don't want a boyfriend yet."

"Right," she said, looking down at her feet. "Thanks for the reality check."

I cringed. Everything I said sounded mean and condescending.

And yet, it wasn't that much off base. We used to say stuff like that to each other all the time, in a jokey sort of way. We could be honest—sometimes really blunt—because we trusted each other enough to know our friendship was solid. Now, without the trust, my words just sounded cruel.

"But when the time comes," I added, "he'll definitely be my first choice."

"You're lucky to have him. As a friend, I mean."

"That's true," I said.

We walked in silence after that, past redbrick town houses shaded by big old trees, their leaves still a fresh spring green; cute little cafés where people sat drinking coffee and talking on their phones; nannies pushing strollers; guys standing on the sidewalk, smoking.

When we got to West Fourth we stopped.

"Tomorrow?" Abby asked.

I felt a rush of relief. I hadn't totally broken her spirit. In fact, Abby was proving to be a lot tougher than I'd ever suspected she could be—tough and totally determined to wear me down and win me back.

"Sure," I said. "Same time, same place."

After she left, I sped up. Being with Abby had distracted me. Now the bad feeling had returned, and I was all on fire to get home and make sure Sofie was all right.

Halfway down the block, a car pulled over. The rear window rolled down and a lady leaned out the window. "Excuse me," she said, "but I'm afraid we're lost." She had a nice, plain face and friendly smile.

"Where are you trying to go?"

"The corner of Macdougal and Bleecker."

"Oh, it's that way." I pointed in the opposite direction.

"We've been driving in circles," she said, sighing. "Can you show me exactly?"

She stepped out of the car and held up her map. It had been folded to the right section. They weren't that far off. I found Seventh Avenue with my finger and traced it down to Bleecker. "Here's Macdougal—"

Then suddenly there was a hand over my face, covering my mouth and nose so it was hard to breathe. At the same time another arm was wrapped around my ribs and I was shoved inside the still-open back door.

Soon the car was moving. Only now the woman who'd asked directions was behind the wheel and another, really ugly lady was pulling a pillowcase over my head. Next she tied my hands and flipped me over so my head was pressed against the seat with my legs hanging down.

When I screamed and struggled the ugly lady slapped my arm hard. Then the radio went on. Classical music, really loud.

"Scream again and I'll do more than slap you next time," the ugly lady said, leaning down, hand gripping my shoulder hard, speaking directly into my right ear. But the voice was wrong. It was growly and low, like a man's.

We drove for maybe twenty minutes. The way I was pinned down—twisted to the side, resting on my shoulder, with my head hanging down at a hard angle—got more and more painful with every bump or pothole in the road.

I would have given anything for a pillow or a rolled-up

jacket—just something to raise my head to a somewhat normal angle. Even an elbow would have done it, if I could have moved my arm. But my wrists were tied with some kind of plastic rope, scratchy and hard. I could feel it scraping my skin every time I pulled or tugged.

In the end I just lay there like a twisted rag, trying not to think of suffocation, feeling the dampness of my own breath settling on my face, and fighting back rising panic. I started to cry, but it was more of a whimper. I didn't have the energy for full-out sobs—and I didn't want to get slapped again.

We drove up a ramp into a parking garage. I could tell by the hollow sound as the tire and motor noise bounced back from the low, hard ceiling. Then the engine and radio were turned off and I was manhandled out, still hooded, and marched up two flights of stairs.

I concentrated on the senses I had—mostly sounds and smells, though I could tell light from dark through the pillowcase and feel the cool of a concrete stairwell on my bare arms.

Our footsteps echoed against the walls. We turned, then climbed, turned, then climbed some more, then finally we stopped. I heard the hollow clunk of a metal door being opened, then I was pushed through the opening and it clanged shut behind us.

We were in a quieter place now, a long hall that smelled of moldy carpet.

The whole time I was there I didn't hear the slightest sound of any other people—no cars, no footsteps, no voices. It was like we were alone in that building, and I couldn't imagine why. Maybe it was brand-new or under construction and hadn't opened yet. But no, I thought, that couldn't be it. The place smelled old, felt old. More likely it was closed and soon to be torn down.

We stopped and I heard a key being fitted into a lock. Unlike our lock at home, this one opened right away. I was pushed inside and plopped down on a molded plastic chair. Behind me I heard a bolt turn.

Then, finally, the pillowcase came off.

I was in a small office with nothing in it but a scratched-up metal desk, some random chairs, and a fluorescent light overhead. There was a window, but the shade was down.

I turned to see the plain lady leaning against the door, arms crossed, standing guard in case I tried to escape. She smiled at me when our eyes met. And despite everything, she still struck me as kind of pleasant.

Meanwhile, the ugly lady with the deep man's voice was pulling off a gray wig. By then I'd already figured it out. Yet somehow it was still a shock to see Lucius Doyle.

He took his time removing the oversize dress. Underneath he had on a T-shirt and rolled-up pants. Slowly he unrolled them, tried to brush out the wrinkles.

He looked entirely different from the man I'd seen in the antiques shop. There, he'd been dignified, quiet—elegant, even, in his three-piece suit and white shirt and tie. Here he was rumpled and ordinary, a man beginning to age and running to fat.

He pulled a chair over and sat down directly in front of me. "Sorry to be so rough," he said, leaning over and brushing at his pant legs again. "I didn't think you'd come otherwise. If you promise to sit still and listen, I'll untie your hands."

I promised, and he set to work on the plastic rope. It took a while. The knot was really tight. When he'd finished, he tossed it on the tabletop.

"I just want to talk, that's all. Then I'll send you home. You want a Kleenex?"

My face was wet with tears, snot, and condensation. I took the tissue and wiped off as much as I could, thinking hard the whole time.

"If this is about the platter," I said, tossing the Kleenex on the ratty table, next to the coil of yellow rope, "I still don't want to sell it. It's my special puzzle."

He gave me a look, like he saw right through me. I guess I'm a terrible liar.

"Just to set the ground rules for our little conversation: I am not stupid. I'm also way ahead of you. Mrs. Berenson called me for advice on how best to repair your platter. I'm the go-to person in New York for antique Dutch porcelain, you see. And now all of a sudden Miss Sofie is walking around Central Park in the flesh. So we can skip all the lies and evasions you were considering just now and get straight to the truth."

I nodded. It had felt like another slap.

"So, how did that happen, exactly? Did you make some kind of wish?"

"Yes. I wished the girl in the picture was my friend. Now she is."

"Thank you for your honesty. No doubt Miss Sofie has been telling you some fantastical tales."

I cleared my throat and sat up tall, trying my best to look him boldly in the eyes.

"Yes, Sofie has told me some things. And for the record, I'm not stupid either. I know who you are. I know you've been watching us. And I know what you did to her."

"Well, well. That saves us some time. Now, I suspect

that Miss Sofie is not exactly happy with her current situation."

"Of course she's not!"

"Just so. But what you may not know is that I also have a difficult situation. That's why I've brought you here: I have a proposition to make. I hope you'll agree that it will solve both her problem and mine."

"Actually, I *do* know about your situation. You made a bad wish and now you're stuck with it."

"Exactly. I propose we help each other."

"And how would that work?"

"You sell the platter to me. I will then change that unfortunate wish. I'll be free to marry"—he glanced over at the woman standing guard by the office door—"and live out my final years in peace. I will do no more harm to anyone. That is a promise. In exchange, I'll release Miss Sofie. She will be just as she was before, back in her home with her family. And that will be the end of it. No more wishes, no more magic. What do you say?"

"I'd rather you released her first."

"Then I couldn't make my wish." He opened his arms wide and shrugged.

I had to admit that was a problem. But I really didn't like it.

"Why do I have to sell it to you? Couldn't *I* just make the wish to . . ."

But I realized, halfway through my little speech, that I'd totally missed the point. It didn't matter who owned the platter. Either way, Lucius Doyle had to go first. Because once Sofie was free, there'd be no more wishing. That left Sofie with no guarantee that he would keep his part of the bargain. He'd already have gotten what he wanted.

I rubbed my wrists where the rope had burned, trying hard to think. "I'll have to discuss it with Sofie," I said. "It's up to her. She has friends who love her and will take care of her, and she might prefer—"

"You know that's nonsense. She's stuck, just as I am. You and your tall friend will live out your lives, grow old, and die, while Miss Sofie will always be a twelve-year-old freak. Trust me, she would *not* prefer to remain as she is."

"I still have to ask."

"Fair enough. Shall we meet again tomorrow? You know it's the only solution. As you said, you're not stupid."

"I'll need more time than that. Tomorrow is too soon."

"You don't trust me."

I actually laughed. "Does that really come as a surprise?"

"Well, you're certainly frank about sharing your feelings."

"You asked."

"All right then, two days. On Wednesday we will meet at Manny's Pizza. Let's say five thirty. Do you know where it is? On Hudson?"

"I can Google it."

"It's a public place. I assume that will be reassuring to you, though I doubt it will be very busy at that hour. Bring Miss Sofie and the platter. I'll take a booth in the back. Just a few words and it'll be done."

"All right. I'll be there. That's all I can promise."

"Good," he said, getting to his feet. "Margo, my dear, it's time we drove young Joplin home."

18

What Happened Here?

I WENT STRAIGHT TO THE Martinellis', where I found Sofie happily watching an old Clark Gable movie while Chloe bustled around in the kitchen. I thought I might faint from relief.

"I called and you didn't answer," I said. "I was really worried."

"I didn't think it would be for me. And I wasn't sure how the phone worked."

"That's what I figured. Can you come down and have dinner with us? We need to go right now. I'm really late and Mom'll be upset. Plus, I have something important to tell you."

"Of course." She got up but left the TV on. Probably didn't know how to work the remote control.

"We're leaving," I shouted to Chloe.

"Have a blast," Chloe shouted back.

Mom opened on the second knock. She must have been waiting in the kitchen.

"You're late," she said. And from the look of her, there was a big storm brewing. After what I'd just been through, I wasn't sure I could handle it.

"I'm sorry, Mom. I had a sort of meeting and it ran late."

She let that pass. It was something else. I could practically feel it thrumming in the air. She'd been sitting there all this time, for maybe a couple of hours, waiting for me to come home so she could dump it on me.

"Want me to help with dinner?" I said, hoping to shift the focus a little. There was no sign of any preparation.

She didn't even bother to respond. "Come with me," she said. "I have something to ask you. Sofie, I'm sorry, but will you please excuse us for a moment?" Then she grabbed me by the arm, in the very same spot where

Lucius Doyle had previously gripped me with his big old hand, and led me to my bedroom.

She placed me in front of the platter. Then she released my arm.

"What happened here?" she said.

I don't know why it hadn't occurred to me that someone might notice the picture had changed. I guess I'd been too distracted by other things.

"Where's Jen?" I asked.

"With Leonard. And stop changing the subject. Can you explain this to me?"

"Um," I said.

"Because it appears . . . Joplin, I looked at that platter very closely. There was a girl standing right there, by the pond. I could describe every detail to you. And I know it wasn't just some decal that was stuck on and could have peeled off."

"That's true," I said.

"And is it just my imagination, or does Sofie look remarkably like the girl who's missing from the picture?"

"Yes. I mean, no, it's not your imagination."

"And what about this?" She reached down and picked up the blue-and-white jumble of clothes that were lying on my bed: Sofie's dress, her apron, and her cap. I'd rolled them into a ball and hidden them deep in the back of my closet, behind my winter boots. Had my mother *searched my room*?

I sighed. All I wanted was to lie down and weep. But Mom continued to stand there holding Sofie's clothes, her eyes a little wild. "You want to *tell* me about this, Joplin?"

"Apparently I have to," I said. But I wondered where I'd find the strength to do it.

"Shall we stay in here?" She lowered her voice and made a little sideways nod in the direction of the front of the apartment, where Sofie was waiting.

"No," I said. "It's her story. She needs to help me tell it. And I'm sorry, Mom, but I really have to sit down."

"Last Thursday," I began, when the three of us were settled in the living room, "the night before I had to go back to school, I was lying there in bed feeling sorry for myself. Because, you know, it felt like everybody hated me. And at some point I looked at the platter, and the girl in the picture seemed to be smiling at me. She seemed like someone who would be really nice, and maybe she was lonely too, like me. I wished she could be my friend."

Once I'd started, it just flowed out of me. I tried to tell things in order, the way Sofie did, and make them sound logical—as much as was possible under the circumstances. The fact that the girl was missing from the picture definitely helped. So did Sofie's Dutch outfit and the bit about Lucius Doyle. My mom had witnessed these things herself. Yet the whole time I was talking, I knew deep down she wasn't believing a word.

When I got to the background part, the things that had happened to Sofie back in Holland, I turned it over to her. She folded her hands in her lap and sat up straight the way she did when she had something important to say, and launched into her story.

"I come from Holland, a small village near Delft," she said, just as she had in Central Park, but she looked directly at my mother the whole time, her expression very grave. She had a soft, sweet voice. You might call it musical, very pleasant to hear. And somehow it seemed more believable coming from her.

Mom listened without making comments or asking any questions. Maybe she was just being polite, but the scowl was off her face for a change.

When we got to the bit about Lucius Doyle and how he was really Hans van der Brock, we told it tag-team fashion. Finally we laid out Sofie's dilemma in all its terrible complexity—and that's where we stopped. I wasn't yet ready to bring up Lucius Doyle's proposal.

For a while Mom just sat there, speechless, shifting her eyes from me to Sofie and back again.

Finally she summoned up a few words. "You realize how that sounds?" It was more of a statement than a question.

"Of course," I said. "I absolutely *do* know how it sounds. But that doesn't mean it isn't true."

There was more silence after that. Mom seemed on the ragged edge of something—exhaustion, despair, her sanity. "I don't know what to make of this. I really don't."

"The girl is missing from the platter," I said.

"I'm aware of that, Joplin. I pointed it out myself."

"And Sofie is here. You noticed the resemblance. You saw her clothes. The little Dutch cap, handmade by her mother."

She shook her head. "It's just too much."

"Sofie?" I said. "Would it be *ethical* for me to use a wish in this situation? A well-meant wish, very small?"

"You are always free to wish."

"I *know* that! I'm asking *you* if it's okay. Will it do more good than harm?"

"Yes," she said. "I think it would help very much right now."

"Good. Mom, I totally understand how you feel. It was hard for me to accept too. But it's real. And if this will make it easier for you to believe—I really *wish* Jen would call and say she's coming home early after all. Um . . . Leonard just remembered some work he needs to finish by tomorrow. And . . . should she bring some takeout from Vin's?"

"Okay," Mom said. Her voice was flat.

We waited. And waited.

It was only a couple of minutes, but it felt like an age. Finally Mom's cell phone rang. Without saying a word she reached over and fished it out of her purse. Her voice was very cautious. *"Hello?"*

A brief silence, then, "Oh. Hi." *Pause.* "That's too bad. Yeah, I know." *Pause.* "That would be great. I haven't actually gotten around to thinking about dinner. Sofie's here too, so get enough for four. Thanks, Jen. Bye."

"Did she mention Vin's?" I asked as she put the phone away.

"Yes, Joplin, she did. You've made your point most eloquently. If this is some kind of delusion, then it's a very convincing one. So, where were we again?"

"We weren't anywhere," I said, "except in the middle of a problem we can't solve."

When the doorbell rang, I leaped to my feet like the rescue squad had just arrived.

"I'll get it," I said.

I peered out the window before opening the door. And there stood Barrett, grinning and holding up a mixed bouquet of flowers, the kind they sell at those vegetable markets that open out onto the street. Only then did I remember inviting him to dinner after basketball practice.

"Come on in," I said. "We need you desperately."

"Excellent. Why?"

"My mom noticed that the girl was missing from the platter. Now it's all out in the open."

"Wow. Did she believe it?"

"Not at first. I had to use a wish as a demonstration. Sofie said it was all right, so don't fuss at me."

"I wasn't going to."

"Good, because it worked. Also, as a side benefit, Jen's on her way home with Vietnamese takeout."

Mom called from the living room. "Who was it, Joplin?"

"Barrett," I called back. "We invited him to eat with us, *remember*?"

There followed an embarrassed silence.

"We completely forgot about you," I said. "But don't take it personally. It's been kind of a stressful day." I got a glass from the cabinet and filled it with water so Mom wouldn't have to go searching for a vase. "Here," I said, putting the flowers in the glass and handing them back to Barrett. "Nice touch, by the way."

"Oh my goodness, Barrett!" Mom said when he gave her the bouquet. "Aren't you endlessly amazing?" She set the flowers on the coffee table and waved with her hand for him to take a seat. "I'm sorry about dinner," she said. "But food is on the way."

"No problem, Mrs. Danforth."

"Mom, Barrett is part of this conversation too. He's known about Sofie from the day she arrived. We've been trying to figure out a way to help her. So it's good that he's here."

But Barrett wasn't listening. He was leaning over and staring, like maybe there was a cockroach crawling in my lap.

"What?" I said.

"That." He touched my wrist right above the thumb, where the skin had been rubbed raw, and the thin, reddish bruise that ran over the top of my wrist. Then he reached across and lifted the other one. It looked more or less the same. "Did somebody tie your hands?"

Mom jumped up like her hair was on fire and came to kneel in front of me. She studied the bruises and scrapes.

"I'm all right," I said.

"Was this some kind of bullying thing? Did it happen at school?"

"No."

I'd hoped to introduce the proposal without telling the whole story, because I knew Mom would go ballistic if she knew. Now it was too late. All the cats were out of the bag and running around our apartment.

"It happened on my way home. Actually"—I took a deep breath—"I was kidnapped by Lucius Doyle."

It was like I'd set off an explosive device in the living room—exactly what I'd been afraid of. Everybody went nuts, like it was the end of the world. Worse, Mom pulled out her phone and started punching buttons.

"Stop!" I practically screamed. "What are you doing?"

"Calling the police."

"No! That would ruin everything! Will you *please* just put that thing down and let me tell you what happened?"

She turned off the phone, but she kept it in her hand. She was going to take a lot of convincing.

"Mom, all he did was talk. He had a proposal to make."

"Where?"

"Where what?"

"Where did this happen?"

"They took me to some empty office."

"They? Took you how?"

"He has a girlfriend. She helped him. We went in a car."

"Where exactly was this place?"

"I don't *know*, Mom. It doesn't matter. Please let me finish."

I wasn't about to mention the pillowcase or the slap. Then she'd call the police for sure.

"All right," Mom said. "But hurry up. I'm having a heart attack here."

"Okay, here it is. Lucius Doyle wants one more wish. Sofie, you were right. He feels stuck and he hates his life. He wants to marry his girlfriend and live out the rest of a normal life with her. He says that in exchange, he'll release Sofie and send her back home to her family. He claims, and Sofie agrees, that he's the only one who can do that.

"But there's one big problem. Doyle needs to go first— because if Sofie is free, she can't grant his wish. Once he has what he wants, he says he'll release her. But we'd have to trust him to do it."

"It's just like the scorpion and the frog."

I groaned. "*Really*, Barrett? *Another* story? Now?"

"No, listen. It's very apt. The scorpion needs to get across the river, but he can't swim. So he asks the frog to carry him. The frog says, no, you'll sting me. And the scorpion says, why would I do that? If I stung you, we'd both drown. So the frog agrees, and halfway across, the scorpion stings him. As he's dying, the frog asks, *why?* And the scorpion says, because it's my nature to do it."

"So this is your roundabout way of saying we can't trust Lucius Doyle?"

"Yes."

"I already knew that, Barrett."

"Sorry. I thought it was pretty good."

"You're *absolutely* sure you don't want me to call the police?" Mom just couldn't let it rest. "The man is a criminal. He should be in prison."

"*Think*, Mom! We need Lucius Doyle. It's unfortunate, but it's true. And if we sic the police on him, he'll never let Sofie go. Please, can't we just try to solve this on our own?"

"Actually," Barrett said, "don't despair!" I swear his eyes actually twinkled. "Once Sofie is safely home . . . *then* you call the police!"

Mom blinked. "Very nice, Barrett. That makes me feel infinitely better."

19

A Family Thing

Mom put on some music. She chose Bach because she said his music always helped her think. But I wasn't so sure about the thinking part. It actually made me feel dreamy and restful, like I was floating over the ocean on a bed of clouds. It must have done the same for Sofie and Barrett too, because we all just sat there and listened.

"You know," Mom said when the first piece was over, "the world is full of miraculous things. I mean, to think that someone long ago could write music like that. We call it genius, but what does that mean? How do you explain it? And then, centuries later, that same music—or the words of Shakespeare, or, I don't know, the sun shining through autumn leaves can spark something inside of us that is far more profound and indefinable than mere logic or reason. Why *shouldn't* there be magic in a world where such miracles can happen?"

None of us had an answer to that question.

The next piece was less dreamy and more cheery. Dancing-around-being-happy music. I was just about to say that while I thought the Bach was awesome, it wasn't helping me think about Sofie's dilemma, when Jen came home. With her came the smell of curry. We heard a rustle and thump as bags of takeout were set on the kitchen table. Then she came into the living room smiling and conducting the music with her index fingers.

"Hi," she said. "What's up?"

Every time we told the story, we got better. Not any more believable, but at least the narrative was clear.

It helped that Mom supported us, and the phone call story nailed it. Jen admitted she'd wondered what had suddenly prompted her to check in with Mom. And it had been ages since we'd gotten takeout from Vin's. It had just popped into her mind.

Naturally, the parts about Lucius Doyle were especially painful for Jen. His status as a bad guy wasn't exactly news by then. But kidnapping me, and most especially what he'd done to Sofie—that really, really disturbed her. And if she had any doubts about that part of the story, the terms of Doyle's proposal erased them. It was as good as an admission of guilt.

"Well," Jen said, "it's beyond strange—but I actually believe you."

"Good," I said, because I had the feeling that if anyone could find a solution to Sofie's problem, it was going to be her.

Or maybe Barrett. It was a toss-up.

"All right, let me ask you something," Jen said, going into analytical mode. "There's something you kind of slid over, and I think it's important: Why are you all so all-fired sure you need Lucius Doyle at all? He might have just *said* he was the only person who could send Sofie home because that gave him leverage to get what he wants. He must know you'd never help him other-wise."

I looked at Sofie. So did Barrett. Jen was right. We'd never even thought to ask.

"Well," Sofie said, "we tried everything else and it all failed."

"Who's *we*?"

"The family I lived with . . . when I was a person before."

Jen gave Sofie a quizzical look. "When you were *what*?"

"A person." She touched her face, her arms, to show that she meant being real and alive, not just a picture on a delftware platter. "Like I am now.

"I'd been trapped in the platter for a very long time by then. No one had ever thought to wish I was otherwise. But then the platter was sold at an auction to a woman who was childless and feeling very heartsick about it. So one day she was looking at the platter and she wished that I were her daughter. It was exactly like what happened with Joplin—she was talking to herself, not seriously believing it was possible. But all of a sudden, there I was, standing in her kitchen."

We all sort of went *huh*—imagining it. And I could see why, this time around, Sofie had decided to appear in the garden instead of my bedroom at night. I might have had a stroke.

"Once she and her husband had gotten over the shock, and once they'd heard my story, they were determined to help me. We decided to do the obvious thing: The mother would *wish* me home. She was the one who had to do it, of course, because the power rests with the owner of the platter, and she was the one who'd bought it.

"So we said our good-byes. She made her wish and I vanished. A few hours later, I called them collect from Amsterdam. Technically, I *was* home, or at least I was in the same place where I'd lived back then. But my family and my home were long gone. It was all concrete, and cars, and shop buildings. So my new mother wished me back."

I let out a huge breath. I hadn't even noticed I'd been holding it. Sofie hadn't told us any of this.

"That was the first failure. Then my new father said that maybe the *wording* had been the problem. Mother should have wished me back to my home *at the time I lived there.* Or maybe even more precise, *on the day before I was first asked to pose by Hans van der Brock.* That sounded like a good guess. It made logical sense. So we said good-bye again, and this time my mother said the exact words—we had even written them down to be sure there was no mistake. But nothing happened. Nothing at all.

"After that, we gave up on sending me home. We couldn't think of any other way. So we settled in and became a real family.

"It wasn't easy for them. They had to rearrange their

lives because of me. But they said they were glad to do it. We moved out to the country, far from other people who might notice things and tell tales. We didn't have company or go out into the world much. And we were schooled at home because I didn't have a birth certificate, no papers of any kind. Legally, I didn't exist."

"You and who else?" Jen asked. "You said 'we.'"

"My sister. She was born four years after I came."

"Were you responsible for that?" I asked Sofie. "The new baby?"

She grinned. "The best wish I ever granted. And for a while, we were all very happy. But after a while we discovered another, more serious complication. It appeared that I was frozen in a particular moment in time. I didn't grow any older and apparently never would. So they couldn't 'raise' me the way parents normally did—teaching me and training me for a future independent life. I could learn things and grow in my mind, but I would always be a child.

"And"—she hesitated here, pulling in a deep breath—"apparently I would go on like that forever. I would never die. You have only to follow that thought to see the many, many problems presented by my situation."

"Oh my God!" Jen said, her hands crossed over her heart.

"Then one day, when I had been with them for eleven years, my mother had a sudden inspiration. She said, 'What if the platter was broken? Do you think *that* might break the spell?' I was amazed we hadn't thought of it before."

"Wait," Mom said. She was sitting bolt upright now. "This mother you've been talking about—*she* was the one who broke the platter?"

"That's right. But this time it was going to be a lot harder to say good-bye. We loved each other very much. And we weren't all in agreement about it, either. My mother felt strongly that it was the right thing to do, but Daddy was against the plan. He was afraid something might go horribly wrong. And to be honest, I think he couldn't bear to let me go. He and Mother argued about it. I heard them late at night when they thought I was asleep.

"And then there was my sister to think about. She knew nothing about my situation. They'd put off telling her because she was so young. It would come as a shock to her, whether they explained it or not."

This part of the telling felt strangely different from the rest, and not only because I knew about the "darkness and forgetting." There was a sudden stillness in the room, like nobody dared to breathe.

"I'm not sure exactly why it happened as it did. Mother was determined to help me. The fact that I didn't grow, couldn't have a future, and would be still as I am now long after all of them were in their graves—it troubled her very much. She thought it was selfish to keep me if there was any chance of setting me free. So she decided to do it when Daddy wasn't around to stop her."

She sighed. "That must have been a hard decision. But she was strong, a person of conscience. So one morning when we were alone she said, 'We have to break the platter now. I'm not sure I'll ever again have the courage to let you go.'"

"Claire!" Mom whispered.

Sofie gasped, and everybody froze.

"It was winter. I was upstairs in my room writing a book report. You were supposed to be doing geometry."

"Anne?" Sofie said.

"You just vanished!" Mom wailed. "You never said good-bye. It was so awful. I thought—oh, such terrible things!"

"Wait, Mom! *You* were the sister?"

She nodded but never took her eyes off Sofie. "It was in the middle of a snowstorm—"

"I remember."

"I knew you couldn't have left the house. Your boots

and coat were still in the mudroom. And there wasn't a footprint or tire track anywhere! There was snow piled up against the doors. But you weren't in the house, either."

She pressed her fingers to her temples, and her voice came out like a groan. *"I thought you were dead. I searched the house for your body!"*

"Oh, Anne!" Sofie scooted over and sat close to Mom, put her arms around her. "It must have been so terrible for you."

"We weren't allowed to bother Daddy when he was working, but I was so scared I went in his office and told him everything—that you had disappeared and Mother was upstairs locked in the bedroom, crying. So he went up there, and I heard them screaming at each other for what felt like hours. And then I was alone in the dark, and after a while I went to my room and locked the door. I even slid a chair under the knob. I was so afraid."

I saw Jen shaking her head—probably thinking, as I was, of that poisonous, secret past Mom had kept to herself all these years. If only she had reached out, explained why she was so sad . . .

"In the morning, Daddy came to my room and I let him in. What else could I do? He said a lot of things that didn't make sense—that you'd 'gone home to be with your *real* family,' that 'it was what you wanted.' I knew he was lying. I mean, I would have known about this 'other family' if you'd really had one. You would have packed up your things, and I would have seen you doing it. You would have given me time to get used to the idea. And you would *never* have gone away without saying good-bye."

"It happened so suddenly, I didn't have a chance. But everything Daddy said was true. And if he'd told you the whole story, you'd have thought that was a lie too."

"I guess so," Mom said. "Oh, Claire!"

I thought back on that week we'd spent in her father's spooky old house, how she wouldn't sleep there, wouldn't go upstairs, didn't want any of his things except his papers. Of course it would be hard for her, going back to the place where her sister had vanished—and she *thought her parents might have killed her*! And Mom was so young then, alone with that terrible thought. No wonder she'd been so miserable and sad.

"When I first saw you," Mom said, "when you walked into the kitchen that day, my hair practically stood on end. Your face, your voice . . . they were so familiar, exactly as I remembered my sister, Claire. But I knew that made no sense at all. She disappeared more than thirty years ago. If she'd somehow survived—and changed her name—she'd have been a grown woman by now. Yet I still couldn't shake the feeling it was you."

"I know," Sofie said. "I felt it too."

At that point, Jen got up and went into the kitchen. Barrett and I followed, leaving Mom and Sofie to their private moment.

Jen started taking cardboard cartons out of the bag and putting them in the microwave two at a time. We all sat around the table, watching the little white cartons going round and round.

"Jen," I said. "Did Mom ever tell you any of those things? That she'd had a sister?"

"No. I knew she was estranged from her parents, but she wouldn't tell me why. After a while I stopped asking."

"Well, if she didn't tell you, she didn't tell anyone, not even Dad."

"Yeah, you're probably right. And to think she carried that terrible pain all these years. Oh, my heart! But what a blessing that you chose that cookie tin to be your special treasure. And then wished that Sofie could be your friend. What an amazing gift that was to your mother, however accidental."

I hadn't thought of that. It made me flush with a strange sort of pride.

The microwave dinged. Jen took out the first two cartons and put in two more. Then I got busy pulling out serving bowls and plates.

Jen found the linen napkins and her grandmother's silver. This was going to be a celebration.

While the last of the takeout was being nuked, Jen cleared the coffee table of everything except the flowers, while Barrett and I set out plates and napkins and silver for everybody. We'd eat on our laps, but we'd eat in style.

Then we brought in the bowls of food, now transformed into a feast.

"Sofie?" I said as we were all scooping beautiful, complicated food out of bowls and onto our plates. "That day in the garden, when you first arrived—why didn't you say your name was Claire?" I remembered how she'd paused to think before answering.

"Because Sofie is my actual name, the one my parents gave me when I was born. But when I appeared in the Camraths' kitchen, they decided to call me Claire—I don't think it even occurred to them that I already had a name. I didn't mind."

I wondered what would have happened if, that day in the kitchen, I had said to Mom, "This is my new friend Claire." Would we have had this same conversation right then and there? And would it have made any real difference in the long run? Probably not. If anything, we knew more now. We were all together, all on the same page, ready to solve the problem. Maybe it was just as well.

For a while we ate without speaking. Just the clink and scrape of forks on china, the occasional little sigh. It felt weird. I was glad when Jen finally found something to say.

"This was meant to be, you know. Before Sofie went home—and we'll make sure she does—she needed to mend something else that broke when your mother smashed that platter. Restore order to the universe, heal some very deep wounds."

Mom looked up and smiled. She looked ten years younger. Like she was glowing from inside.

"And I hope this isn't rushing things, Anne. But it's getting late, and I suspect Barrett needs to go home pretty soon. But more important, in two days Joplin and Sofie have a meeting with that terrible man. We need to decide how they're going to handle it.

"As it happens, I've been considering the matter, and I think I have a really good idea. Shall I tell you?"

"*Of course!*" we all said. "*Please!*"

"Okay. This is a *bargain* Lucius Doyle wants to make— call it a deal, an agreement. He will do *this* if you agree to do *that*. Only, it's tricky because you don't trust the other party to keep his promise. In a situation like that, who do you call?"

I wanted to say, "Ghostbusters?" But I said, "I don't know."

"Leonard!"

"Why?"

"Because he's a lawyer, honey, and a very good one. He's going to write us an airtight contract that will cover every possible contingency."

"Like what?" I couldn't imagine.

"Well, let's say you grant Lucius Doyle the *temporary and fully legal* ownership of your platter for a period of exactly ten seconds, but only on the stipulation that he uses it to make a *single particular* wish—he'll put in some language about exactly *what* wish can be made and how it must be worded—after which Mr. Doyle agrees to release Sofie from her bondage. And in the event of his failing in this aforementioned duty, his rights to said platter and the powers it possesses will be retroactively rendered null and void, with all the advantages of said ownership lost, destroyed, abandoned, and blah, and blah, and so on.

"If Doyle's magic has logic and laws and he signs that contract, then he *has* to fulfill his promise or he'll lose what he's gained."

"I don't believe it!" Barrett said, boggle-eyed with admiration. "She fixed the flaw!"

"You always were my guardian angel," Mom said. "Now you're Sofie's too."

"Thanks, honey. I *am* sort of floating on air."

"Me too," I said. "And I think I speak for all of us."

20

The Letter of the Law

LEONARD HAD PROMISED TO BE at our apartment at eight thirty sharp the next morning. He had a meeting at ten he couldn't miss, but he thought the contract sounded simple, probably no more than a single paragraph of well-crafted legal prose. It should take less than an hour to discuss. We could give him all the details when he arrived.

I couldn't wait for *that* conversation. Little did he know what he was in for.

We were all a little giddy and exhausted that morning. Sofie's couch-cushion bed had been set up in Mom's room instead of mine, which was fair, I guess. But every time I woke, I wondered where she was. Then I would remember, turn over, re-fluff my pillow, and lie there staring into the darkness for a while. Each time, I would hear voices floating from the front bedroom. I guess they had a lot to talk about.

Finally, just before dawn, I fell into a deep sleep. So when the alarm rang I woke in a panic, desperately trying to remember everything and wondering if there was something important we'd missed.

I waited till seven fifteen. I assumed that anyone with a job or kids who needed to get to school on time would be up by then. So I called Barrett and pretended I was letting him know I'd be missing school again. I didn't want him to search for me in the library and worry that something bad had happened.

He said he'd actually figured I'd stay home, considering all that was going on. He'd drop by the apartment after chess club, though he'd pass on dinner. Apparently his parents had started making comments, like Barrett was beginning to fade from their memories, he'd been gone so much lately.

Just before hanging up, I asked my real question: *Was there anything we'd forgotten?* Any little loophole we'd failed to consider that Lucius Doyle could slip right through? No, he said. He'd thought about it long and hard, and if Leonard was as good as promised, the plan should work like a charm.

I went back to getting dressed, wondering what you were supposed to wear to a meeting with a big-time lawyer—not at his office but in your own apartment. In the end I went with a sundress and flats. I even fluffed my hair the way Jen did, but it just hung back down the same old way the minute I stopped fluffing.

It was then, as I was standing in front of the mirror, feeling dissatisfied with the consistency of my hair and the amount of space between my eyes, that it hit me like a punch: Abby! We were supposed to meet at the corner.

I checked the clock. It was almost eight. She'd be standing there already, waiting for me. And she would probably go on standing, doggedly waiting, till it was absolutely clear I wasn't coming and, if she didn't hurry, she'd be late. Her heart would shrivel up with pain because she'd think I'd done it on purpose. That I'd set her up for a fall: ha-ha-ha!

"Where are you going?" Mom asked. "Our meeting's at eight thirty."

"I know," I said. "Be right back."

"But—"

She was probably going to say something about Lucius Doyle and how I shouldn't be going out alone. But I didn't hear it because I was already out the door—sprinting up Perry Street, hanging a left on West Fourth, dodging a very startled woman, flying over the leash connecting the woman to her little dog, and reaching the corner about six minutes past our usual meeting time.

Abby was there, stiff and small, waiting for me.

"Sorry!" I said, gasping.

"Are you all right?"

"Yeah." I bent over to catch my breath. "Ran the whole way."

She looked confused. "You forgot your backpack."

"I know. I'm not going to school today. There's something going on at home. Nothing bad, but I need to be there. I'll be back tomorrow."

I saw it dawn on Abby then. "You ran all the way over here just to tell me that?"

"Yeah. I said I'd be here. I didn't want you to think I . . . well, you know. I didn't want to stand you up."

"Oh," she said. I saw it cross her face: the realization that I was, at least in some very small way, still her friend. That I cared enough to run five blocks at breakneck speed to keep from hurting her feelings. "You are *so* amazing."

"Nah," I said, kind of embarrassed. But it felt good to hear her say it. "Anyway, gotta go. See you tomorrow?"

"I'll be here."

And then I was off again, sprinting back toward home. I met the same woman with the little dog. This time she saw me coming, scooped up her fluff ball, and stood cowering with her back pressed to a deli's plate-glass window.

I waved at her as I went by. I felt like a million bucks.

I got home ten minutes before Leonard was due. Mom was standing at the door, hand on the knob, peering out the window. I could see she was upset with me and had been stoking the flames the whole time I'd been gone.

"It was important, okay?" I said. "Have a little faith." And I trotted off to my room.

I'd sponged myself down and changed into another, nonsweaty sundress by the time Leonard arrived. I was glad I'd bothered, because he wasn't his usual khakis-and-Hawaiian-shirt self. This was expensive-lawyer-in-a-custom-made-suit Leonard. A whole different creature.

We sat in the kitchen because he needed the table for taking notes. "Think of it as a conference room," he said with a grin.

Once he was settled, legal pad out and pen in hand, he turned to me.

I had to go first because I knew the most. I was the one who'd heard Lucius Doyle's proposal. And Sofie and I were the ones who'd have to meet with him the following day.

I launched into my story and tried really hard to be clear. But I was nervous, and pretty soon I was deep in the weeds. So Sofie jumped in to help. Then Mom or Jen would notice things we'd left out and come to the rescue. You might call it a group effort.

Leonard was amazingly patient. He listened very carefully and didn't ask many questions, but the ones he asked were good. And he made only one snide remark: "I'm just going to pretend this is all real, and concentrate on the letter of the law."

"I think that would be wise," Jen said.

After that, if we'd told him we needed him to add a clause preventing the ogres from kicking the fairies out of their sublet, he would have found a way to do it.

"Okay," he said, checking his watch. "We finished? Anything else?"

"One small but important request," Mom said, looking at Sofie. "We were talking last night, and I'm afraid this will have to be done in two steps—the meeting tomorrow to sign the contract, with the understanding that the actual transaction will occur one week later. Sofie and I—and Joplin—need a little more time."

"I doubt the other party will like that."

"So do I. Nevertheless . . ."

"Okay, Anne. I'll write it in. I'll make it very specific: that you will complete the transaction at such and such a place and time or the contract will be rendered null and void. That should reassure him. If you don't follow through, there's a penalty for you as well."

"Make it exactly the same, just one week later," Mom said. "Five thirty at Manny's Pizza. He chose the location, so he'll feel comfortable with that."

Leonard nodded and wrote on his yellow pad.

Then he put the pen down and did a weird thing with his mouth, sucking in his lips and pressing down. It was like he had a serious concern with something we were doing. He glanced over at Jen and they silently agreed.

"I have to say, I'm a little uncomfortable with this," he said.

My stomach lurched. "Why?"

"Because, from what you've told me, this man is—how should I say this delicately?"

"Is a criminal?" I suggested.

"Yes. This is a man who forced an eleven-year-old girl into a car and took her to some abandoned building to make his proposal."

Worse than you know, I thought. That didn't even

include the pillowcase over my head, the rope, the slap, and the hard hand gripping my arm.

"Now he insists that Joplin and Sofie meet him *alone* in a pizza joint—without an adult. I don't like it."

Mom flushed. I knew she felt the same but didn't think we had a choice. Now she was embarrassed that Leonard had to be the one to point it out.

"What do you suggest?" Mom asked.

"That you and I be present at the meeting. Not Jen. He knows her. But it's a public place, after all. We'll get there early and order pizza. How is he to know we aren't ordinary patrons? I suggest you dress down. I'll do the same."

"Thanks, Leonard," Mom said. "That's beyond generous."

"Like hell it is," he said. "This is *family*. Jen, once I get this done, I'll messenger two copies of the contract over to you at Christie's. I'll drop by here after work tonight to make sure you've approved the language. Okay? All done?"

"Um," I said. Everyone looked at me. "One last thing? I'm just hoping—I mean, Lucius Doyle isn't a lawyer or anything. He's an artist and a shopkeeper. I'm sure he's read a lot of contracts before, like when he rented shops and stuff. But people get nervous when they see a lot of legal mumbo jumbo—"

"Mumbo jumbo!" Leonard said. And then he laughed—really, really hard.

"Was that rude?" I asked.

"No. It was very astute. Doyle is not expecting a contract. That's going to throw him off right from the start. If he doesn't understand what he's being asked to sign, he'll think you're trying to pull a fast one on him."

"Right."

"Actually, Joplin," Sofie said, "he may be a potter and a shopkeeper, but he's also really smart. He had these big, old books on alchemy and other dark arts—he *taught* himself Latin so he could read them. And he's had a long, long life since then to learn things, maybe even law. Whatever we do, we shouldn't underestimate him."

Leonard nodded. "Well said, Sofie. It'll be a good contract, I promise. Bulletproof, shockproof, waterproof to ten fathoms, belt and suspenders—and in *plain English*. It's a simple agreement and you have nothing to hide. All you're asking the man to do is what he's already promised. You just want him to play fair."

"Phew," I said.

Leonard folded the pages of his legal pad back down, slipped it into his briefcase, and got to his feet. "I'll see you this evening," he said, leaning down to give Jen a kiss.

This time I didn't mind at all.

21

Do or Die

BARRETT WALKED WITH US MOST of the way. We were all pretty nervous.

Two copies of the contract were tucked in beside the platter in a sturdy canvas bag. The platter was protected by layers and layers of Bubble Wrap. And in case Doyle insisted on actually laying his eyes on it, I'd added some scissors for cutting away the tape. I asked Mom to buy the kind they use in preschools, with blunt tips. I didn't want him to think I'd brought a weapon.

Actually, there was no point in bringing the platter at all. We wouldn't be using it that day, assuming Doyle agreed to our contract. And the following week, when we did the actual wishing, it didn't really need to be there. Ownership was the only thing that mattered. But he'd said to bring it, so we had.

It made me nervous, though. I was afraid I'd trip and drop it, and then it would break, and Sofie would disappear into darkness and forgetting. I couldn't get that out of my mind.

"If it broke, you'd just get it fixed again," Sofie assured me.

"I know." But I clutched the handle even tighter. So tight my fingers were starting to go numb.

We stopped at the little park in Abingdon Square, where Barrett would wait for us. We sat on one of the benches over by the World War I memorial. It's this big bronze statue of a soldier holding a giant flag.

"I'll be right here when you're finished," Barrett said. "You okay?"

"I'm fine," I said—then realized he was talking to Sofie, not to me. And she didn't look fine at all.

"I'm just scared, that's all," Sofie said. "I haven't seen him up close since that day—well, you know. And the thought of sitting down across from him . . ."

Her arms were folded across her middle, hands tucked

under her arms, the way you do when it's cold. She was trying to calm herself.

"I hope you'll do the talking, Joplin. I'm not sure I can."

"I will—but if you think I'm saying the wrong thing, just give me a nudge. And we'll be in a public place, remember. Mom and Leonard will be there. And I still own the platter. If it gets scary, I'll make a wish."

"You didn't when he grabbed you," Barrett said.

"I know. It never even occurred to me. It's just not something I'm used to doing. I'll remember this time, though. I promise."

Barrett checked his watch. "It's time," he said. Then he raised a long, skinny arm like a priest giving us his blessing and said in a deep Obi-Wan Kenobi voice, "May the force be with you."

As we headed up Hudson toward Jane Street, I took Sofie's hand. It was damp with sweat and she squeezed mine hard. She was clearly terrified.

Up ahead was a faded awning in a color best described as dirty red. Somehow I knew this was going to be the place, and sure enough it was. Lucius Doyle had picked the most nondescript, unappealing, walk-right-by-it-without-a-glance pizza parlor in the whole West Village. As we got nearer, the smell of garlic nearly knocked us over.

"This is it," I said.

Manny's had a big picture window in front with the name written on it. And inside, sitting across from each other in a middle booth, Mom and Leonard were sharing a pizza.

They were the only customers in the place.

"He's not there," Sofie said.

"That's so weird. You think maybe he's in the bathroom or something?"

"Could be." But she sounded doubtful.

I was doubtful too. If Lucius Doyle wasn't there, it meant he'd decided not to come. And that was the one possibility I hadn't even considered, because it made no sense at all. He was the one who'd set up the meeting.

I gasped, then, as a hand clutched my arm just above the elbow and jerked me away from the window.

"Change of plans," said Lucius Doyle as he performed a quick adjustment, switching the gripping hand from his right to his left so he was free to wrap the other arm around me. Now it looked less like he was dragging me away and more like he was giving me a fatherly embrace as we walked down the street together. The canvas bag hung down between us, tight and awkward, bumping against our legs.

Margo and Sofie were in front of us, leading the way. Margo had hooked arms with Sofie in this really insistent way, squeezing Sofie's elbow firmly against her ribs. Sofie turned to look back at me, panic in her eyes. But Margo gave her a tug and muttered something. Sofie turned back around.

"Why are you doing this?" I snapped to Doyle. "We followed your exact instructions."

He snorted but didn't respond.

There were people around, but nobody seemed to notice us. I guess it's a New York thing: you ignore the crowds, give one another space, pretend the other people aren't there. Unless, of course, they're dressed like Godzilla and handing out flyers, in which case you totally avoid them.

We weren't that interesting—though we would be if I decided to scream. Then somebody would definitely notice. They might even try to help or call the police. On the other hand . . .

I didn't have time to make that decision. Everything happened too fast. Just up from Manny's was a gray metal service door. This time Margo didn't even have to pause to pull out a key. It was already unlocked.

So this had been planned in advance, which made no sense at all. Why set up a meeting, then change the place?

The door led to a dank, dim entry space with a row of black plastic garbage bags leaning against one concrete wall. I wondered how they had access to all these weird, empty, ugly buildings. Maybe Margo worked in real estate.

Straight ahead was an elevator, the old-fashioned kind with walls of metal grating. Probably designed for moving freight.

Doyle slid the accordion door open and pushed us inside. Margo pressed a button, then the elevator made its noisy, grinding way up to who-knew-what.

"Please," I said. "This isn't what we agreed to."

"Didn't I make myself clear before?" His voice was so low and so hard, it cut through me like a blade of ice. "I am *not* stupid."

"I know that."

"You really didn't think I'd recognize your mother? Also the man, who has visited your apartment many times?"

I didn't have an answer for that. He was right. Totally.

"Were they there to protect you?"

"Yeah."

"That was very foolish."

The elevator stopped. We stepped out into an L-shaped storage room with shelves on the walls stocked with cans, bags, and boxes. A tower of cardboard cartons waited to be unpacked. Brooms and a mop leaned in a corner, next to a giant bucket on wheels, a washer and a dryer, a dirty-looking refrigerator, and a freezer chest.

I figured we must be directly above Manny's Pizza. So probably there was some other access to the restaurant, maybe a stairway that led to the kitchen. But we couldn't see it. Margo turned in the other direction and opened the door to another dingy office. Except this one looked like it was being used for actual business.

"Sit," Doyle said. Once again he took a place behind the desk. I guess it was a power thing.

Sofie was as white as a corpse. I tried to get her to look at me, but she didn't move, just went on staring at the floor. "It's okay," I said, reaching out and touching her arm. She nodded but still didn't look up.

"Are we going to do this?" Doyle said.

"Yes," I said. "Absolutely."

"Let me see the platter."

I hesitated. "It's all wrapped up. And it's still mine for the moment. You don't have the right to demand it. That wasn't part of our deal."

He tilted his head and gave me a look. "Aren't you full of yourself!"

"No. I'm scared. We're both scared. But I still get to stand up for myself and Sofie."

"Just show me the platter."

"Why? It's covered in Bubble Wrap and packing tape. It would be a hassle and a waste of time to unwrap it. And there's no point. I'm not even sure why you asked me to bring it. The platter could be on the moon and I'd still have the power to make wishes. Or to sell it to somebody else, who could then make wishes. As you well know."

"I like to see what I'm getting."

That sounded like an opening. "You don't trust me, then?"

"Of course I don't."

"Thanks, because Sofie and I don't trust you either. I'm not saying that to be obnoxious. I'm making an important point."

"Which is?"

"We both want to make this deal, right?" He was drilling me with his eyes, trying to see into my brain. *Right?*

"Yes."

"So how can we make sure that both of us are being honest and fair?"

He gave me his stone face. So I reached into the bag, pulled out the contracts, and set them side by side on the desk.

The silence that followed was like a *thing*, a misty ghost that had slipped in under the door and had now expanded to fill the room, pressing us down. It was like a roaring in my ears.

"It's a contract," I finally managed to say. "Two identical copies. One for you and one for me. All it says is that we will both do what we agreed to do—what you *already offered* to do. The only change to your original proposal is that we want a little more time so we can say good-bye to Sofie. It's going to happen, I promise. Sofie wants this even more than you do. And, thanks to the contract, you won't *have* to rely on my promise, because I'll sign—"

"Please stop talking."

I sat up straighter, gripped my hands together in my lap, and pressed my lips together.

He was looking down at the two contracts. I saw him glancing from one to the other, making sure they were identical. The ghost of silence grew heavier in the room, sucking out the air. It was hard to breathe. I could hear my heart going *rump-a-tump-thump*.

Margo went over and stood almost directly behind him. And in a sort of embrace, she leaned down, one hand resting on the desk on either side of him, her cheek almost touching his as they read the contracts together. It was odd to see them like that, Lucius Doyle and his lady love in an affectionate pose. It made him seem almost human.

It didn't take them long to read. Margo went back to her chair.

Sofie was shivering now and I was scared again. What if he refused? It occurred to me that I could do something like what I'd done to Chloe—*wish* him to sign it. But then I thought, no, that would be forcing him to do it. And if he didn't sign of his own free will, the contract might be invalid. I didn't know for sure, but it wasn't worth taking the chance.

"How many people know about this?"

"Just my family."

"The man sitting with your mother is not part of your family."

"Yeah, he is. He's engaged to Aunt Jen."

"Who is not your aunt and isn't part of your family."

"She is too!"

"What about the boy?"

I nodded. "He knows."

"The little girl with the red hair?"

"Abby? No. Absolutely not."

"The neighbor with the hair and the tattoos?"

"Nobody else at all! Not a single person! And I only told my family because I had to. They didn't even know the truth about Sofie until that night. I said she was our neighbor's cousin. But then I came home late from school with rope burns on my wrists and Mom went ballistic. She wanted to call the police. I had to explain why she shouldn't."

Lucius Doyle thought about that. He stared into space, mechanically stroking the back of his right hand with the left, fiddling with his rings.

I turned to Sofie and this time we locked eyes. I raised my brows, trying to send a message of faint but real hope. She pulled her head down into her shoulders, like a turtle retreating into its shell.

"Also," I said, "Mom saw us looking in the window, so she knew we were there. Then we disappeared and you didn't show up. I told her what you did to me before—though I made it sound a lot less awful than it really was, because that would have made things worse. And she has a cell phone. She may already have called the cops. I hope not, because that would really mess things up."

That first part was a lie. Mom actually hadn't looked

up. But the rest was real. We were late, and she'd be worried.

Doyle thought about it for a few seconds. Then he pulled out his own phone and handed it to me. "Call her."

"What should I say?"

"Everything's all right. Your mother is not to worry, just stay where she is. You'll be there in a minute."

I took the phone and punched in her cell phone number. I did it slowly because my hands were shaking. She answered on the first ring.

I tried really hard to sound normal and follow the script I'd been given. But Mom didn't make it easy. She kept asking questions that were hard to evade, like "Where are you?" I could hear the panic in her voice.

"Mom, *please*," I said, cutting her off. "It's fine! Just hang in there. We'll see you in a minute."

I hung up and handed the phone to Doyle. He slipped it back into his pocket.

"I don't like this," he said. "But I understand it."

And without another word, he produced an expensive-looking pen. And in real ink, in beautiful script, he signed his name.

22

Old and Wise

JACKSON SLOAN HAD A BEACH house on Long Island, near the town of Bridgehampton. He let us stay there for a few days—just Mom, Sofie, and me.

Actually, he did a lot more than that. He sent a limo to pick us up and take us out to the house. And when we got there, toward evening, we found fresh flowers in all the rooms. And on the kitchen island there was this big tray of food, like at a party. Four kinds of cheeses, fancy crackers, figs and pears, grapes.

And that was just for starters. The fridge was stocked with salads and lunch meats, clam chowder and Bolognese sauce. We could have stayed there for weeks and never run out of food.

Based on the limousine—which I later found out wasn't Jackson's at all, just something he hired to be super nice to Mom—I was expecting his house to be really grand and decorator perfect. Like Abby's ginormous pile on Martha's Vineyard, which I'd never actually seen, but Abby had described in disgusting detail.

But it wasn't like that at all.

True, the house was big. It'd been built a long time ago for the Sloan clan to gather in the summers—grandparents, aunts and uncles, cousins, and their friends from school.

I could imagine all those squealing little kids playing croquet on the lawn, running in and out from the beach with sand on their feet, wet towels draped over the porch railings, toys and sand shovels lying on the steps.

Grandma Sloan would be sitting on the covered porch in an Adirondack chair, looking out at the ocean, a straw hat on her head and a book in her lap. Meanwhile, someone in the kitchen—maybe Jackson himself—would be cooking up a pot of fish stew for dinner.

The house seemed full of happy ghosts and good memories. And everything about it felt right—the sound of the waves and the wind, the damp, sometimes chilly air, the sun on the dune grass. The cozy little bedrooms with wonky ceilings and dormer windows with cushioned seats. The crayon marks on the wallpaper.

It was the perfect place to spend our last few days together.

Mom had met with the principal on Thursday morning. She'd explained that, due to a "family situation," we'd be away from the city for a while. She was fully aware that I'd already missed nearly two weeks of school, but we needed these few more days. After that, Mom promised I'd work really hard to catch up. She'd get me a tutor if that would help.

Mrs. Chaffee had been amazing. She'd acknowledged that it had been a difficult time for us, and she regretted that the school situation had made things worse. She said it wasn't a problem if I missed a few more days. And when I came back, if I needed help with my schoolwork, St. Mark's would make sure I got it.

I let Abby and Barrett know we'd be gone for a while. Then we left that same afternoon and stayed till the limo picked us up again on Monday.

We waded in the surf, but only up to our knees because Sofie didn't know how to swim. And besides, the water was cold.

In the basement we'd found a collection of little plastic

buckets with tiny rakes and shovels to go with them, along with a fair amount of last summer's sand. We made a sand castle using the little kids' toys, but the tide took it overnight.

Sofie tried to make something philosophical out of that, along the lines that life is fleeting and precious, and we should accept the beauty of every moment. I didn't really want to go there, to be honest, but Mom got tears in her eyes. And then I did too. However much I knew it was right, it was hard to say good-bye, knowing I'd never see Sofie again.

We got teary a lot while we were there. It was a really emotional time. But I could tell that, despite everything, Mom was happy. It wasn't like before.

She had her phone out constantly, not to make calls but to take pictures of Sofie and me—splashing water, posing behind our castle with our toy shovels, wearing funny hats, posing in front of the house.

She said they'd never had any family photos when she and Claire were children, not even of Christmas or birthdays. Now she understood why. It would've been too obvious that Anne was growing and Claire was not. It would have been Claire with the infant Anne. Claire looking just the same with four-year-old Anne. Claire still the same when Anne was seven. But because there were no pictures, *not a single one*, it meant that after Claire disappeared, there hadn't been anything to remember her by. And memories fade with the passing of years.

Mom was making sure that wouldn't happen again. These pictures would be printed and put in frames. We'd look at them every day.

The first three days, the weather was nice, so we spent a lot of time on the beach. Mom would take pictures and we'd collect shells: scallop shells in all different colors, from white to yellow, brown, and red, always with the delicate ridges that fanned out like a sunburst. Sturdy clamshells, which we mostly left behind. And the delicate little moon shells, gray as the sand and forming a perfect spiral. Strangest of all were the jingle shells—little odd-shaped, wrinkled flakes that looked like an old man's toenails, if toenails were made of shining, golden mother-of-pearl.

There were mermaid's purses—fat black packages with four thin spikes. Mom said they were the egg cases of sharks. There were crab's legs everywhere, and seagull feathers.

We collected them all. When we got back to the house, we'd wash them and lay them out on the kitchen island to admire.

On the second day, Mom said we should each pick our

favorite shell. It would be a sort of beauty contest. But pick a small one, please.

We went back and forth for a while. It was hard to choose just one. But in the end we both went for scallop shells. Mine was pale pink with darker pink on the ridges. Sofie's was yellow, almost orange at the base, growing lighter as the shell fanned out, with tiny spots of orange against white along the edge.

Once we'd made our choices, Mom carried them downstairs to the basement. Twenty minutes later, when she came back up, she'd drilled little holes in the bases so we could make them into necklaces.

We wore them constantly after that. We called ourselves the Shell Sisters.

But more than anything else, wherever we were or whatever we were doing, Mom and Sofie talked about their past. "Do you remember?" they'd say, over and over.

"Do you remember the stars we pasted on your ceiling?" Mom said. "And you insisted that all the constellations had to be absolutely correct, just like in your star book?"

"Do you remember," Sofie said, "when we made that snow fort and you wanted to capture a rabbit and put it in prison? And I said it would be too hard to catch one. Also, the rabbit would probably jump right out. And even if it didn't, it would be mean to the rabbit. So you put your toy dog in prison instead. Then you left it there, and it snowed, and we didn't find the dog till spring?"

I was like the fly on the wall, listening as their secret past was revealed for the first time. I knew how important it was. They were mending an old wound, setting the story straight.

It turned out that Mom actually had a happy childhood—for the first seven years, anyway. She didn't know how strange and isolated their little world was. It seemed perfectly normal to her. She had a wonderful sister, who was also her best and only friend. And she adored the parents she later came to think of as monsters.

Like all parents everywhere, they had made mistakes, mostly having to do with Claire. Then, like my teacher Mr. Crocker, they'd made matters worse by handling the situation badly. After that, things fell apart.

As a result, my mom had rewritten the story of her childhood to make it dark and grim. Now, little by little, her long talks with Sofie were bringing back the real, true story. The good parts.

It was like opening the big French doors in the back of Jackson Sloan's house and letting in the ocean breeze, so it could scurry around the rooms, rattling papers and stirring the flowers. It always made me feel clean and full of hope. That's what they were doing.

I was happy for my mother and for Sofie too. But I had my own pain to deal with. It was like I'd already lost Sofie to Mom. Soon I'd lose her completely. She'd disappear into the past, and the moment she vanished, she'd already have been dead for hundreds of years. It made my insides quiver just to think of that. I'd never, ever see her again.

But at least I had my mother back. I cried over that too.

Our last night in the beach house, we had pasta Bolognese. The sky had been threatening all day, and toward evening it started to rain. We shut all the doors and windows. After dinner, Mom made a fire. We curled up in the living room on these cushy old sofas with their faded flowered slipcovers and piles of mismatched pillows, watching the flames and talking.

I hated the thought of leaving. Everything had been so perfect, and now it was almost over. "If only we could stay here like this forever," I said, "exactly the way we are. Wouldn't that be great?"

"No," Sofie said, softly but in a way that I knew she really meant it. "Nothing lasts forever. It would get stale after a while, like a shut-up house. This is perfect because it's a moment. You will always remember it."

"Okay," I said. "It's nice that we had such a wonderful time together in this beautiful place. Is that better?"

Sofie smiled. "Much."

"And nice of Jackson to let us come," Mom reminded us.

"Yes, it was. Amazing. But why did he invite us in the first place? I mean, it's not summer or anything. It's a totally random time. It seems kind of weird."

Mom smiled. "Not at all. He knows about Sofie, and he thought we'd want some time together in a peaceful place. So he offered this house."

"You *told* him?"

"No." Now the smile was a full-on grin, positively merry. "My father did. Those boxes and boxes of papers of his—turns out, they were all about Sofie, though he called her Claire, of course. Apparently he wrote about her, and nothing else, for the last thirty years of his life. I think it became his reason for living.

"I was trying to do the same thing myself, with the memoir. I wanted to capture my sister on paper, everything I could remember, so there would be a record that she'd walked this earth. But my memories were those of a very young child, without nuance or understanding.

"I'm glad my father did it properly. Jackson says, from what he's read so far, it feels like a grand nineteenth-century novel. It starts in Holland and carries her forward till the day she disappeared. A saga, I guess you'd call it."

"How much have you read?"

"Not much. Jackson set some pages aside for me, just

to give me the big picture. But they were still cataloging the boxes. And by the time there was anything to read, I was at home—you know, because of what happened at school. Still, I've read enough to know it's a book about a girl named Claire who never ages and watches the world unfold over hundreds of years. It's got these wonderful little details. Honestly, it's like being transported back to Holland or old New York, but in very particular rooms where you meet very particular people. You can practically hear the clock ticking.

"But it wasn't till the other night, when I asked you about the platter and Sofie started telling her story, that I put it all together. I realized that Daddy hadn't just used Claire's name. The girl in my father's book *was* my sister. She really *had* been ageless and timeless, which is why she'd had to leave. And now, by some miracle, she'd returned to me.

"So, to answer your question: That's what I told Jackson—that Sofie was Claire, that she'd come back, and that we were going to bring her saga to a happy end."

Sofie was stretched out on her own couch, propped up with pillows, her pale hair spread out like a mermaid's, quietly listening and staring dreamily at the fire.

"Do you want to read it?" I asked her. "The book?"

She nodded. "We're going up to the office when we

get back. I'd like to see how he told it, but I already know the story. I'm the one who gave it to him. The story and all the details.

"I'd be telling him about something and he'd break in to ask me questions. You know, 'Where was the window—was the light coming in from behind or the side?' 'Tell me about the table setting, the dishes and the food.' 'What were the sounds from outside—horses and wagons, people selling things on the street, dogs barking?'

"That's when I felt closest to him. We hardly saw him during the day. He was always working. Then there was dinner and family time. But often after Anne went to bed"—she looked over at Mom—"we'd sit up in the living room and talk for hours. Mother too, but not that often. I think it made her sad to hear about my past. She thought of it as suffering.

"But I was glad to tell my stories, to reimagine those moments completely. It helped me hold on to what I'd learned from the many houses I lived in, the moments I'd witnessed, all the people whose lives I watched." She sort of drifted off at that point, like she was sleepy. Or maybe she was just soaking up more details—the flickering light of the fire, the soft pillows, the smell of sea air and tomato sauce.

"I'm glad he asked those questions and wrote

everything down," I said. "What you told us in the park—that was just an outline. I want to know the rest."

"I'm glad too," Sofie said. "Daddy will have told it better than I ever could. The way his mind worked, he was always digging deeper, looking for meaning. He asked me what was going on in my mind during those long days and longer nights, when I was looking out at the same wall, the same room, and nobody was there.

"And you know—I was surprised, once I started trying to remember, how much thinking I'd done. How I'd changed over time. I'm not the same person who posed for Hans van der Brock. I look like her, but I'm older and wiser."

"Have you thought," Mom asked, "how it'll be when you go back home—being so changed, and accustomed to the comforts of modern life?"

"I think about it all the time. That, and other things too. As a girl in that world, I'll be kept in my place. And I want more than that. I'll finally get the chance to lead a full life, and I want to do something important with it. I want that for Greta too. I'll teach her to read. And if she can't go to school, then I'll teach her myself. I'll need to take it slowly, though. If I just walk in the door one day and start making changes, my family will think I've lost my mind. But if I'm careful, I think I can help them all have a better life."

"I have no doubt of it," Mom said.

"Sofie?" I'd been playing with a thought for a while now. This seemed the moment to say it out loud. "If you can—I mean, I don't know how you'd do it, but maybe you can figure out a way . . ."

"What?"

"Could you leave us a message? So we'd know you got home safely, that you still remembered it all. That you remembered us?"

Sofie thought about that, staring at the fire. "Something that would last into the future."

"Yeah. So there's some chance we might actually find it. I know that's a tricky assignment."

"Don't worry, Joplin. I'm old and wise. I'll figure it out."

23

A Force to Be Reckoned With

On Tuesday night, we had dinner at Jackson Sloan's apartment, our whole little support group—Mom and Jackson, Jen and Leonard, Barrett, Sofie, and me. It was the last time we'd all be together, so Jackson went all out.

There were candles in old-fashioned candlesticks, the kind that had lots of arms. There were flowers, and lacy napkins, and beautiful china and glasses. All these things looked old, like maybe they'd belonged to Great-Grandma Sloan.

They'd probably been stored away for years. I mean,

what does a single guy need with lacy napkins? But he'd brought them out for us.

There was music playing softly in the background. I was pretty sure he'd picked the Bach especially for Mom. Probably the flowers too. When she saw them, she said, "Oh! Peonies!"

I bet he already knew they were her favorite.

He turned the lights down low, so once the sun had set the room was lit by candlelight. And out the windows we could see the twinkly lights of the city.

Like our wonderful days at the beach house, it was perfect. I wouldn't have changed a thing.

Now the final day and hour had come.

Mom stayed home with Jen keeping her company. She and Sofie had already said their good-byes in private. And this time apparently they did it right—nothing left unsaid, no mysteries, no regrets.

The rest of us walked up Hudson in a tight little knot, Barrett on one side and Leonard, carrying the platter, on the other. We reached Abingdon Square and stopped in the same spot as before. Only this time, the mood was different.

Sofie wouldn't be coming back.

We stalled for as long as we dared, till it was absolutely time to go. Leonard leaned down, gave Sofie a kiss on the cheek, and whispered something in her ear. Whatever it was, it made her smile.

Then Barrett scooped Sofie up in his arms, lifting her off the ground and swinging her around, leaning into her hair to hide his tears. Finally, after what seemed a very long time, Barrett let go.

Then Sofie and I went on together, holding hands. She looked back only once and waved.

As we neared the pizza place, it occurred to me that Leonard (or Jackson) might have hired someone to watch us this time, some guy who *looked* like a slacker but was really a private detective.

If there was such a person, it turned out he wasn't needed. When we got to Manny's, Lucius Doyle was already there, in the back booth by himself. A small pepperoni pizza was sitting on the table, untouched. I saw no sign of Manny or any of his waiters. We were completely alone.

When we sat down, Doyle pushed the pizza tray aside, up against the shakers of parmesan, the pepper flakes, and the shiny napkin holder. I set the delftware platter down in the space he had cleared, and cut away the wrapping with my kindergarten scissors.

I didn't do it for Lucius Doyle; I did it for myself. I wanted to make sure that when Sofie disappeared, she didn't return to the platter, trapped again for all time.

"Are you ready?" he said.

We nodded.

The exact timing was important. The contract gave him only ten seconds. So he laid his phone on the table with the stopwatch feature open. "Say whatever good-byes you need. Let me know when you're done."

"We already have," Sofie said. She seemed strangely confident all of a sudden. Her moment had arrived.

"All right," I said, following the script, "I transfer ownership of this platter and all the powers that go with it, for the purpose of making one wish only, according to the contract we have both signed. Your ownership begins *now*."

Doyle pressed *start* on the stopwatch. Numbers flew by on the screen.

"I hereby reverse my wish for immortality, so that I may grow old gradually, in the manner of mortal men, beginning as I am now, at this time and place, in middle age."

He looked down at his phone. His time was up. The platter was mine again. But it didn't really matter. The rest was up to Lucius Doyle.

We waited while he pulled three plastic baggies out of his pocket. Each had powder of a different color—yellow, white, and blue. Just as Sofie had described.

"Hold out your hands, palms up."

Sofie did.

"You're sure you remember how to do this?" I asked.

"Please." His voice was cold and hard. "Don't talk any more."

I was sitting close to Sofie, our shoulders touching. I could feel her leg warm against mine. She gave me a little nudge. It felt like a smile, but her face was solemn.

Lucius Doyle was speaking softly in words I couldn't understand. I stared at him as he worked his magic, opening one bag at a time, sprinkling the powders over Sofie's soft, small hands, and making a mess on the table and the platter.

I stared at him the whole time, as Sofie had on that terrible day when he first enslaved her. I remember that his face was square and compact, except for the jaw, which was starting to droop. I looked at his skin. It had a sheen to it—maybe oil, maybe sweat. His lashes were pale and stubby. There was a mole on his cheek, right beside his mouth. The nose had a sort of ball on the end, like what happens when you squeeze the tip of a balloon. It was pinker than the rest of his skin.

He didn't look like an artist, a person capable of painting something as beautiful as my platter. Nor, for that matter, did he look like a man who would teach himself Latin so he could read forbidden books. He looked like a merchant, a seller of cloth. Maybe a cobbler who made boots.

The last powder now, just a pinch of the blue. I couldn't distract my mind any longer. I leaned against Sofie a little harder, feeling the warmth of her real-person body, saying good-bye.

And then, where she had been, there was nothing. It was what I'd expected, but when it happened it shocked me. My heart lurched inside my chest and I felt a cold wave of sorrow sliding over me. But I was determined not to cry in front of Lucius Doyle, who was brushing the powder off his hands and mopping it up with paper napkins, as though what he'd just done was nothing.

I picked up the platter and stared at the picture for a couple of beats. It was still just a landscape with geese, a pond, some trees, and a distant windmill. Sofie wasn't there. She'd gone home. I stuffed the platter and wads of wrapping into the canvas bag. Then I slid out of the booth.

"You know, I could call the police right now," I said. "I could tell them about the kidnapping. That's what my mother wanted to do. They'd probably put you in prison, where you could grow old behind bars. But I said no, because then I'd have to see you again, and hear you tell lies in court, and I didn't think I could stand that."

The look he gave me was cold yet strangely lacking in expression. He didn't even bother to thank me.

Barrett and Leonard were waiting outside the restaurant, just far enough from the window that Lucius Doyle wouldn't see them. Now they wrapped me in their arms, like I was an accident victim, and ferried me away toward home. I can only imagine how we looked. Neither of them said a word till we had turned the corner.

"Was it okay?" Barrett asked. "Is it done?"

"Yes." I started trembling, just thinking about it, and they were all over me again.

We shuffled along like that for a while. Then I kind of shrugged them off.

"I'm okay now," I said, handing Leonard the bag and taking Barrett's hand. "Let's get out of here."

I knew I wasn't okay, not yet. I'd dream of that moment—when Sofie's warm touch turned to empty air—for years, maybe for the rest of my life. Then I'd wake and remind myself it was *good*, it was what Sofie wanted.

But the thing was—it had been so *real*.

After a while, Leonard hung back and left Barrett and me to walk by ourselves. That was nice. It helped. And it gave me a chance to ask a question that had been troubling me for a while.

"Do you think she'll actually remember us? Because if she really went back to be the person she was before she met that monster on the road—wouldn't she be the same innocent girl who let him trick her into posing?"

Barrett let go of my hand and hooked his arm in mine instead. That brought us closer. I felt his warmth where Sofie's had been. How he'd known that's what I needed, I can't imagine, except that he's really smart and a wonderful friend.

"If it was that simple, then Lucius Doyle couldn't be sitting in a New York pizza parlor four hundred years in the future. He'd be back in Holland smoking his pipe and preying on innocent girls. I think time has its own shape; it's not a river that runs only one way, but more like a circle or some other complicated shape. I think Sofie is back there right now with her three-hundred-plus years of wisdom, her whole life ahead of her, and lots of big plans. And you know what?"

"What?" I said, or I *sort* of said it, because I was letting it all hang out by then, heaving big sobs and wiping my face with my free hand.

"She's going to be a force to be reckoned with. That little Dutch village won't know what hit it—but I promise it will never be the same."

Postscript

THREE YEARS LATER

I WAS IN MY ROOM doing homework when the phone rang. Mom was still at Sloan, Hart. She had an office there by then, and only one book to edit, with lots of help from Jackson Sloan.

I got up and went to the living room, thinking it was probably Mom saying they were going out to dinner, and would I mind ordering in?

But it wasn't Mom, it was Jen.

"Hi!" she said, with this semicrazed enthusiasm that put me on alert. Clearly she had something big to say.

"Hi back. You sound weird."

"I am! I can hardly contain myself!"

"Well then don't!"

"I have to! At least until tomorrow!"

We really *did* speak in exclamation points. It was that kind of conversation.

"Okay—so what happens tomorrow?"

"You and your mom ditch whatever you have planned—"

"Like my algebra test?"

"Yes! To hell with algebra! Tomorrow at ten is as long as I can wait. You and your mom. At Christie's. At ten!"

"Is Leonard there? Do you need an intervention?"

"Nope! I'm just ducky!"

And she hung up the phone.

Seconds later it rang again.

"What?" I said.

"Barrett too!"

Click.

We were up at Rockefeller Plaza well before ten. Mom had her cup of iced coffee. I had my backpack so I could go straight to school after my "doctor's appointment." Barrett had on a jacket and tie. He said he had a feeling it was called for.

Jen hopped out of a cab and ushered us inside. She looked pretty much the way she'd sounded on the phone. And she was moving us along so fast we couldn't ask what was going on. We just trotted along behind her.

All right, I'll be honest here. I had a feeling too.

Waiting at the elevator was Jackson Sloan. He gave Mom this raised-eyebrow questioning look. She shrugged. It was a mystery.

Jen showed her pass to a guard, who unlocked a room.

As she ushered us in, I could see her hands were shaking. She looked ready to explode.

"This is a showing for an upcoming auction of minor Dutch paintings of the Renaissance," she said. "These aren't Rembrandts or Vermeers, you understand, but gifted painters all the same. *More affordable*," she added, shooting Jackson Sloan a significant look. Then she mouthed *wedding present!* so broadly that even the guard could have read her lips.

We let three or four seconds pass before Mom said, *"Jen!"*

"Okay, okay! So there's a lot of great work here, and I was going through it yesterday after the paintings had been uncrated and were being hung . . ."

All of a sudden she was sobbing, right there in the

Christie's viewing room, like she was having a nervous breakdown. Clearly this was something she couldn't handle. So she just grabbed Mom's hand and led her across the room. We followed behind them like sheep.

She stopped in front of a small painting. It showed a woman sitting at a table beside a leaded glass window, light streaming in. In front of her on the table was a wooden stand and on the stand was a picture. She held a paintbrush in her hand. But she wasn't looking at the picture; she was looking out at us.

Actually she was probably looking at herself in a mirror, since this was a self-portrait. That's how they did it back then, before they could work from photographs.

But the really interesting thing was that the artist was a woman—unusual for the 1600s. And judging by her clothes and what we could see of her house, she must have been doing pretty well for herself.

All of this washed over me in perhaps two seconds, because my eyes had gone straight to her face—the creamy skin, the sweet smile, and that remarkable halo of pale blond hair.

Jen was still sobbing uncontrollably. Seconds later my mother was too. The guard was getting nervous. Barrett was practically cutting off the circulation in my right arm. And for a moment I wasn't sure my legs would hold me up.

Because, lest there be the slightest doubt: hanging around the artist's neck, suspended from a golden chain, was a scallop shell.

Acknowledgments

When I was very young, I moved with my mother from Abilene, Texas, to New York's Greenwich Village, where we lived in a basement apartment on Perry Street. The apartment backed onto a spectacular garden that ran the whole length of the block, with winding walkways, boxwood hedges, stone statues, ivy-covered walls, and burbling fountains—utterly magical and quite unexpected in a big, noisy city.

My parents had divorced early on, so it was just Mother and me—a tight little family of two. She was young then, still in her twenties—glamorous, flamboyant, and delirious with joy to be out of small-town Texas and living a Technicolor dream life in the Big Apple. Her friends were poets, painters, and actors. They listened to jazz and talked about literature and art. I wanted to be just like them.

Famous people were everywhere. I watched Mary Martin fly across the stage as Peter Pan on Broadway. The poet Dylan Thomas came to one of Mother's parties. She met the artist Jean Miró through a friend, and I still have some of his beautiful prints. Eleanor Roosevelt, who lived near Washington Square Park, allegedly took a fancy to me when I was taken there for walks. And I got to be in the "peanut gallery" on *The Howdy Doody Show*, where I met Buffalo Bob and—my hands-down favorite character—Princess Summerfall Winterspring.

It was a strange life for a little girl, certainly not what you'd call normal, but while much of my childhood has faded from memory, I could tell you a thousand stories about the New York days. They ended when Mother was diagnosed with tuberculosis. She had to go away for treatment, and I was sent back to Texas to live with family. Things were never quite the same after that, which of course is why I remember it so vividly. It was a golden world, since lost, a world my mother, with her bright spirit, magically gave to me.

While we were still living on Perry Street, Mother wrote her first book, a murder mystery set in our apartment. When, years later, I too became a writer, I often thought of using that lost world in a book of my own. But I couldn't seem to find a story to go with the setting. Then an old idea about a magical Chinese bowl and a boy who gets trapped in time began to shape-shift in my subconscious. The bowl became a delftware platter and a new story line emerged.

I wrote several chapters and a loose outline and sent them as a proposal to my editor, Rosemary Brosnan. At that point I already had my characters: a mother and her daughter; their wonderful roommate, Jen; and a precocious boy named Barrett Browning. I had my setting: the apartment, the garden, the Village, and the school I attended. And I had the broken shards of a delftware platter in a cookie tin. But the story itself—about the girl's father, who returns from a POW camp after the war—was still pretty vague.

Rosemary liked the proposal. And having worked with me for years, she already knew that the plot would change—probably drastically—as soon as I started writing. And she trusted me to change it in a good way. But she did make one stipulation: the book should be set in modern times, not the 1940s.

That was a blow. I had already done an enormous amount of research. I knew when the POWs returned from Europe and the ships they traveled on. I knew what was playing on Broadway at the time, what a dress would cost at Bergdorf's, and exactly where Eleanor Roosevelt, who would somehow fit into my story, was living.

But what troubled me more than the wasted research was the prospect of writing a contemporary story. I didn't want to write about kids who were always texting and tweeting and taking selfies. That stuff is so *not* magical.

But I gutted it up and got to work, trying to adapt what remained of my plot to the world we live in now. And I quickly discovered that letting go of historical constraints freed me to follow my imagination wherever it wanted to go—to write a book not about history but about family, friendship, and loss, secrets and misunderstandings, kindness and second chances.

Which leads me—*finally*—to the acknowledgments. With her unerring wisdom, my ever-astute editor, Rosemary, opened the door to the book I really needed to write. So, heartfelt thanks for guiding me and trusting me all these years, and for being such a kind and generous friend.

Copious thanks to my husband, Peter, who listened to hours of my dinner-table dithering as the plot was coming together, who read the manuscript numerous times, and who suggested that maybe a painting could be the message from Sofie at the end.

Many thanks to my fabulous agent, Marcia Wernick, for being there whenever I need a bit of sage advice or moral support. And I'm grateful to the good-hearted members of my writers' group—Marc Talbert, Ashlee Glasscock, Mark Karlins, and Mary Lee Updike.

Finally, though Joplin's story is completely different from the life I lived on Perry Street, the themes that run through it are deeply personal and very real. I realize now that this whole book has been a love letter to my mother, and a celebration of that wild and glorious together-time we had before she got sick and everything changed.

So I would like thank my mother, Fay Grissom Stanley, for being such a wonder and for teaching me so much. You formed the person I became, opened my eyes to a world of possibilities, made me a writer, and taught me how to love.

Fay Grissom Stanley
Perry Street apartment, 1950